L'AMOUR EN NOIR

A SCREENPLAY COLLECTION

by

Rich Etienne

ISBN: 9781718175839

AUTHOR'S NOTE

Due to the unique nature of the book's printing, you may get a defective copy.

If so, send pictures to brokeartistgallery@gmail.com and I'll ship you a new one.

To

Yakko, Wakko, and Dot

CONTENTS

PREFACE

I write screenplays.

I've tried so many openings for this preface, but none of them worked. The first was so pretentious, when I read it, I actually cringed, curling my upper lip to block my nostrils. The second went on this existential, yet hollow, rant about what it means to be a writer, with even more pretension sprinkled on top. And the third opening looked a little like "asfbifhiashf" from when I bashed my head on the keyboard in frustration.

No more. I'm cutting to the chase:

I write screenplays.

I've written web articles, poems, three short novels, mini-bios for blogs, comic books, song lyrics, and a nauseating amount of Instagram captions for photographers, where I just wanted to put "It's not that deep-- shut up and double tap" (sorry, Lou).

Despite all the many formats I've written for, none of them comes remotely kinda-sorta close, down the block and around the corner to the sheer joy I get from writing a 30 to 110ish page screenplay. It's not just the joy of completing such an arduous task. It's the entire process. It's the joy of sitting there all hours of the night, the darkness bleeding into morning, knowing daggone well I've got work in three hours, punching out on my keyboard a slew of scene headings, action beats, scene transitions, and best of all... dialogue. Honest-to-goodness, right-there-on-the-page, short-but-sweet, long-but-meaningful dialogue-- with not a single one interrupted by "said he" or "she laughed" or "he said as he entered the room".

I wrote my first screenplay when I was 6 years old. Can't say I remember what it was, and I definitely can't say it was any good, but knowing me, it was probably a musical. I was always a storyteller, using mostly illustrations and short prose, but my life changed completely in 1998 when I saw a two-part episode of Steven Spielberg's ANIMANIACS.

Yes. You read that right.

Yakko, Wakko, and Dot had just finished writing their 800-page screenplay and set off to pitch it to the Warner Bros. CEO, Thaddeus Plotz. Hilarity and musicality ensued, complete with Hollywood references that went over my head as a kid, but make so much sense to me now. It was right there, watching those episodes after school on KIDS WB!, eating Ritz crackers and drinking Mott's apple juice that I decided I was going to write screenplays, too.

As of my writing this, my first screenplay, as short as it probably was, was completed 20 years ago. I've been writing screenplays consistently ever since.

Granted, I wasn't exactly great, or remotely good, or even particularly competent for the majority of those 20 years... but the passion was always there. In the back of my head, there was the idea that I could one day write my own 800-page epic, and sing a song and dance a dance to pitch that screenplay to Thaddeus Plotzes everywhere.

Well, that hasn't worked. So, let's try this instead.

This is L'AMOUR EN NOIR, translated from French to English as "Love in Black". A collection of film noir short screenplays filled to the brim with the best the genre has to offer: hard-boiled detectives, dangerous dames, blood guilty gangsters, and best of all... love at its worst. Love at its most painful. Love in black.

A world where the shadows of Venetian blinds cuts across your face and stabs into your heart. A world where every ray of light is, in actuality, a shimmering blade that with one fell swoop, cuts you off at the knees, leaving you in the gutter, half a man, bleeding out.

I love noir. Real and true noir. Nowadays any story with so much as a detective in it is classified as noir in the same lazy manner that the Ray Charles movie is sometimes classified as a musical (just because it has music in it, does not make it a-- you know what? Never mind). But, noir-- bona fide noir? That's the kind of storytelling I live for. Where every character, be they male or female, cop or robber, citizen or politician, is weighted by their past, struggling with their present, and doing everything they can to avoid the inevitability of their future. I've taken in noir in every format I could: from movies like CASABLANCA and THE MALTESE FALCON; to comic books like BLACKSAD and Darwyn Cooke's adaptation of Richard Stark's THE HUNTER; to any of the numerous episodes of BATMAN: THE ANIMATED SERIES, and its theatrical debut MASK OF THE PHANTASM, where one of its characters served as inspiration for a screenplay included here: SANDS MARQUEE.

And for the record, "bona fide noir" is both Latin AND French in the same phrase, and I'm more proud of having written that than I should be. But hey, with stories as dark as these, some levity is required here. And by dark, I mean dark. Not violent, gritty, or bloody. But dark. The absence of light. The intangibility of hope. And what better way to write those stories, than with love at the center of them?

I'm not against love. I love, and I love hard. And despite its repetitively less-than-expected outcomes, I'm more than ready, waiting, and wanting to love, love hard, and fail again. Every time I start jonesin' for a hit, pull out that pack of fatal attraction, light up a small white tube of romance, and take a long, deep puff of late night texts and inside jokes, I always bear in mind the Surgeon General's Warning:

LOVE CAUSES SHORTNESS OF BREATH, HEART PALPITATIONS, STUTTERING, AND ACTIN' BRAND-NEW IN FRONT OF YOUR FRIENDS. DO NOT LOVE THE WRONG PERSON AT THE WRONG TIME, NEITHER THE RIGHT PERSON AT THE WRONG TIME. AND FOR THE SAKE OF GOD IN HEAVEN ABOVE-- DO NOT LOVE SOMEONE WHO DOES NOT LOVE YOU BACK, OR EVEN WORSE... LOVES SOMEONE ELSE. (Trust me, that last one is a kick in the teeth)

I read that warning every time I take a smoke. "It won't get me", I say. "I've cut down to three packs a day. I'm good." My lungs are black, my fingernails are yellow, but my heart? Still going. Still pumping. Takes a lickin' and keeps on tickin'.

And that's what I love about noir. Life can be a meat grinder for the characters, but they never give up. No matter how uneventful the last investigation, they investigate another. And if they're fired from the police force, no worries, they become private dicks. No matter how many times they're told to "stay out of official police business", they keep digging for further clues.

And most importantly, no matter how many dames break his heart, no matter how many pigs use her and throw her aside... they never forget to fall in love again. Sure, they say they want nothing to do with it. Sure, they speak short and harshly to anyone with baby-blue or hazel-brown eyes, and have late night rendezvous with Jack Daniel's and his good pal Jameson. But, despite their words, and despite their actions, even if they never get into another relationship ever again, their heart does what it always does. Their heart does what it only can.

It loves. And in life, you learn more about a person (or character) when they're rejected or denied, than when they're accepted or granted.

You've probably never read a screenplay before. And that's fine. I am humbled by being your first. You probably looked at the page count and thought there's no way you'd ever get through this. Trust me: the pages of a screenplay are NOTHING compared to the pages of a novel. You'll do more than fine. You'll excel at this.

It'll be awkward at first. But a few pages in, and you'll get the hang of it. You'll instinctively recognize the Scene Headings, and put together that

INT. ABANDONED BUILDING- DAY

means we're looking at the INTerior of an abandoned building during the daytime, and that

EXT. ABANDONED BUILDING- NIGHT

means we're looking at the EXTerior of that building at night. Should you ever see

(FLASHBACK)

then guess what? You got it. That scene is a flashback.

You'll realize that the parenthesis under a character's name in all-caps describes how the character is saying that dialogue. You'll be able to feel that...

                    BILLY
          Yeah. I'd love to go shopping at Ikea
          with you.

...is so much different from...

                    BILLY
                  (scoffs)
          Yeah. I'd LOVE to go shopping at Ikea
          with you.

You'll know that the word "beat" means "pause"... that "(V.O.)"
means "voiceover", somebody narrating... and that "(O.S.)" means
"off-screen", a character speaking, well... off the screen-- you
can't see them yet.

You'll understand that FADE TO or DISSOLVE TO or CUT TO or
even SMASH CUT TO are simple scene transitions that are,
thankfully, self-explanatory. They aren't immediately
important for the reading experience, but they can elevate the
way you film the scenes in your mind.

And most of all, when you read "END", you'll know that the story
is finished, and believe that you've spent intimate time with
characters that despite not being real in our world, they've
managed to be real in your heart.

Corny, I know... but that's the experience I get when I read
stories. And it's that same experience I'm here to share with
you.

At the end of the day, my screenplays are nothing more than
words on paper-- words very near, and immensely dear to my
heart. The product of my heart, in fact. So, if they cannot be
produced then, at the very least, they deserve to be read.

So, here they are.

My name is Rich Ahavah Etienne.

I write screenplays.

FADE IN:

INT. INDIGO'S APARTMENT- LIVING ROOM- DAY

A MAN and WOMAN stand side-by-side before an open LIQUOR
CABINET. A box of liquor in his hands. They laugh and
giggle as they arrange the alcohol on the shelves.
Playfully nudging each other.

INDIGO and CHESIL.

SUNLIGHT flushes in through the uncurtained windows.
The apartment is bare. Just moved in. A baby-blue polo and
khakis for the slim, stringy Indigo. A simple white dress
for the long-legged, figure-8 Chesil. Happy couple.

Chesil pulls a bottle of RED WINE from the box. We see her
RING: Cheap. Dime a dozen. But its sentiment sparkles in
the sunlight, making it priceless.

Indigo takes her hand. Kisses it. Then her arm. Her
shoulder. He goes for her neck. She shrieks, giggling.
Drops the red wine into the box, which falls out of his
hand, and--

KSSHHH! They step back as the bottles SHATTER. Wines and
spirits billowing out. Chesil cuts Indigo a playful look:
"See what'cha did?"

Indigo looks at the mess before them. Smiles. Kneels down
to the broken glass, and picks up the same bottle of wine.
It's the only bottle that didn't break. Chesil smiles at the
sight as he hands it back to her.

                    CHESIL
          Should probably take it as a sign. Save
          this for something.

Indigo puts his arms around her waist. They look at the
bottle as if it's their child. Their future.

3

                    CHESIL
            Not sure what. Guess we'll know when it
            happens. Something rare and special...

She looks into his eyes. Sunlight bouncing off his
glasses.

                    CHESIL
            ...or maybe something simple.
            Something foolish.

Those last words resonate with Indigo. Like a cherished
memory. He gently takes her chin. Kisses her. And we...

                                        FADE OUT

We're surrounded by BLACKNESS. Much longer than we care
to be.

LIGHT flashes in as a WHITE SHEET is pulled off us,
revealing Indigo. Dark coat, dark shirt, dark pants.
Almost matching his skin. Cold, empty eyes. Hands in
pockets. Beside him, is GARCÍA : dress slacks and buckled
trench.

They look down at something. At US. She waits before she
asks:

                    GARCÍA
            Is this her?

Beat. Long and painful. An eternity passes. Indigo just
barely nods. García motions to someone off-screen...

...and the WHITE SHEET returns. Taking us to BLACK.

INT. CITY MORGUE- HALLWAY- NIGHT

Tile floor and marble walls. A long stretch of cold gray. A
RUNNING AIR VENT hovers over Indigo. He sits on a steel
bench. Looking at CRIME SCENE PHOTOS. His stringy body,
slouched. García stands before him.

THE PHOTOS: A cramped apartment. Furniture overturned,
vases shattered.

                    GARCÍA
          Landlord found her, trying to collect
          the rent. Full autopsy is gonna take a
          while. Won't know what killed her till
          then, but...

BLOOD on white carpet. A huge, frightening puddle.

                    GARCÍA
          ...those bruises make a pretty strong
          argument. Don't think Tyson could've
          walked from that.

A close up of a delicate, female HAND. Limp. Bruised.

                    GARCÍA
          A man was seen leaving her building.
          Running like he saw the devil himself.
          6'1, maybe two. Dark overcoat.
          Eyewitness had stepped out to shut off
          her car alarm. Working theory is the
          alarm scared him off. Forced him outta
          dodge.

A door separates the long hallway. Through the door's
window, a young woman listens closely. Taking notes.
Short and spunky. Sloppy dresser. Thanks to the INK on her
hands and mouth from her pen, they call her SQUID.

Indigo flips through photo after photo. Taking
everything in. Not once looking up at García.

                    GARCÍA
          She was writing a letter.

He stops. Looks at the RED ENVELOPE García holds out.

                    GARCÍA
          To YOU, apparently. That's how we got
          your address.

5

He takes the Envelope. Puts it in his breast pocket. Goes back to the photos. Stares at the blood stain.

> GARCÍA
> There was a framed photo of you and her in the apartment. How long were you together?

He doesn't answer. Eyes covering every inch of the crime scene photo.

> GARCÍA
> How long since the break up? Saw some other envelopes, same size and color... Was that her thing? Or just for you? You guys keep in touch?

Indigo's thumb softly caresses the image of the limp hand. Trying to get one last touch.

> GARCÍA
> She tell you about any enemies? Anyone who would want to do this to her?

He doesn't say a word. Frozen. Locked onto the photos. García glances over, see Squid by the door.

> GARCÍA
> Hey! Are you kidding me, right now?

Cover blown, Squid walks through. Hungry.

> SQUID
> Not here to ruffle any feathers. Just looking for a couple scraps. Any possible leads on who might've--

> GARCÍA
> This is NOT the time, Squid.

> SQUID
> Okay, let's schedule a time. Couple questions, I'll be brief.

                    GARCÍA
        Squid. OUT.

Squid surrenders. Pockets her notepad and leaves.

Indigo flips to the FINAL PHOTO. Another shot of the blood
stain. His eyes follow it to its source. Passing a
SHATTERED FRAMED PHOTO of him and Chesil. Passing more
red envelopes. Finally, his eyes rest on a BOTTLE.

                    GARCÍA
        ...You okay, sir?

The "blood" is red wine. THE red wine. THEIR red wine.

                    GARCÍA
        Sir. Are you okay?

The air vent exhales on the back of Indigo's neck. In his
eyes are pain. Torture. Death.

                    INDIGO
        I'm cold.

We EASE IN on the photo. See the bottle is marked PINOT
NOIR, and we...

                                            FADE OUT

INT. THE JOINT- NIGHT

Smoke, haze, booze, and babes.

POP! A SPOTLIGHT explodes onto RICKY GORDON. Tux and bow
tie. He's been told he's handsome far too many times.
Actually believes his hype. He counts off the BAND onstage
with him. They begin the beguine and Ricky croons into
the mic.

EXT. THE JOINT- NIGHT

PATRONS wait on line. Excited to get in. Indigo crosses

                        7

the street and cuts the line. Heading for the entrance.
Hands in pockets. Just as he reaches the door--

--a bouncer blocks him with his arm. MOE. A body like a
cinderblock. His brain, too. He points to the other
patrons: "There's a line".

Indigo doesn't care. Doesn't even look at him. Goes for the
door once more. Moe's arm budges not an inch. He pushes
Indigo off. Indigo's eyes keep to the ground. Hands still
in pockets. Holding back.

Two more bouncers emerge: LARRY and CURLY. The three
surround Indigo, expecting an easy slaughter. Smiling.

Indigo's eyes cut up at them. From the rim of his glasses, a
look like a bullet. He takes his hands out.

Their smiles die.

INT. THE JOINT- NIGHT

The AUDIENCE snaps along with Ricky. Savoring each and
every note. Seated at the bar, is Squid. Holding an OLD,
WRINKLED FLYER of Ricky singing and dancing... with
Chesil.

"RICKY GORDON-- FEATURING CHESIL AMOUREUX! A DUO LIKE
NO OTHER! LIVE AT THE JOINT!"

Squid watches the performance. Waiting for the right
moment, until--

KROOM! Moe CRASHES through the front door. Unconscious.
The audience gasps. Squid whips around to see. The band
stops. The guy working the SPOTLIGHT quickly turns to get
a look, accidentally putting the spotlight--

--right in Ricky's eyes. He squints. Can't see a thing.

                    RICKY
          What's... what's going on?

All he hears: FOOTSTEPS. Tables and chairs OVERTURNING.
Dishes CLATTERING. Patrons GASPING.

                    RICKY
          Boys? Boys, you out there? What's--?

From the WHITE GLARE that pierces Ricky's eyes, a
SILHOUETTE emerges. A BLACK HOLE in the form of man.
Immediately, Ricky knows.

                    RICKY
          Indigo... Listen for a second.

The silhouette GROWS CLOSER. Ricky tries to keep his cool
for his audience. Each FOOTSTEP and CLATTER inflates the
lump in his throat.

                    RICKY
          Indigo, listen. Okay. Let's sit down.
          Let's talk, let's--

Indigo MATERIALIZES from the ether of the spotlight.
Ricky turns, running to:

INT. THE JOINT- BACKSTAGE- NIGHT

He trips on a wire, crashing to the floor. Quickly turns
on his butt. Scooting away. Indigo advances on him. An
encroaching lion.

                    RICKY
          I didn't do it. It wasn't ME.

Indigo's breaths are ragged. Peppered with snarls.
Kicking crates and trunks out of the way. Fingers
flexing: Open, then curled. Open, then curled.

                    RICKY
          Indigo. LISTEN. It WASN'T me.

Ricky backs into a corner. No escape. Indigo closes in.
His hand reaching for Ricky's face, when--

                         RICKY
          IT WASN'T ME!

Finally, Indigo hears. He freezes. Everything is quiet.

                         RICKY
          I know... I KNOW what you're thinking,
          but I swear to GOD it wasn't me. I
          haven't spoken to her in almost a year.
          Not since we broke up.

SHRIPP! Indigo yanks Ricky's phone from his pocket.
Taking fabric with it.

                         RICKY
          Okay, okay! Yes, I called her, left
          messages-- plenty of 'em. I mean, you
          know how she was. Those eyes, that
          face-- can you blame me, she was one
          fine broad!

Indigo cuts him a look.

                         RICKY
          WOMAN! She was a woman! Look, I'll
          admit, when we broke up, I was hurt.
          She broke my heart, not to mention
          cracked me upside the head. But, think
          about it: If I wanted Chesil dead, you
          think I'd wait this long to do it? You
          think I'd still be around, show my face
          in public? ONSTAGE?

Indigo SHATTERS the phone on the floor. Doesn't want to
hear it. Ricky finches. Desperate to prove his point
before it's too late.

                         RICKY
          LISTEN to me! I know who you are, man! I
          know how you handle things, how you
          get things done! If I wanted her dead--
          if I REALLY wanted her dead-- you
          wouldn't have had the chance to find
          out about it. Cuz I would've emptied my

        bank account hiring every finger with
        a trigger to make sure YOU were dead
        FIRST.

Beat. That sits with Indigo. Makes sense.

                    RICKY
        If it's one thing I know... it's how much
        she means to you. What you would DO for
        her. You can say I'm a dog, you can say
        I'm scum of the earth, and you'd
        probably be right. But, you can't ever
        say my momma raised a fool. I didn't. Do
        it.

Indigo stares him down. Burning holes through his
glasses, into Ricky's soul. Breathing through his nose.
Ravenous for answers. For payback.

EXT. THE JOINT- BACK ALLEY- NIGHT

WHAM! WHAM! WHAM! Indigo UNLEASHES on a garbage bin.
SOMETHING must face his fury. Again and again, he attacks.
Until he can no more.

He drops to his knees. Releases a BELLOWING HOWL.
Anguish. From the depths.

Squid looks on from the back door.

Tears stream. Lips quiver. Indigo's breath stops short.
Eyes bulging. Grabs his chest. He goes for his pocket and
pulls out a bottle of PRESCRIPTION PILLS. Also from his
pocket, falls out the Red Envelope García gave him.

He pops the pills. Chews them, no time to waste. As he
controls his breathing, trying to calm... his eyes focus on
the Red Envelope. Memories flood back.

As if she's right there, he hears her VOICE:

                    CHESIL (V.O.)
        Careful. Pills and liquor'll kill you.

EXT. APARTMENT- TERRACE- NIGHT (FLASHBACK)

Standing by the terrace wall, Indigo finishes taking a sip of whiskey. Turns to see Chesil stepping out. Both dressed in black. They're at a WAKE. On the terrace with them, is a table with chairs and a TABLETOP GLASS FIREPLACE.

Indigo rests his pill bottle on the wall. He's just taken a dose.

                    INDIGO
          You talk with experience.

                    CHESIL
          Not me. I mean, I KNOW... but I don't
          really care to find out.

                    INDIGO
          Isn't that the same thing?

                    CHESIL
          Not in the least.
                    (then)
          So. Out here, all alone... I take it
          you're not a fan of funerals?

                    INDIGO
          Is anyone really?

                    CHESIL
          Don't see why not. I mean, anything
          that starts with the word "fun" should,
          at the very least, be SOMEWHAT
          enjoyable.

Chesil lightly bumps into the chair. Indigo holds back a small laugh.

                    CHESIL
              (to chair)
         Pardon me, madam.
              (to Indigo; extending hand)
         Hi, I'm tipsy.

They shake.

                    INDIGO
         Indigo.

                    CHESIL
         ...I don't get it.

                    INDIGO
         That wasn't a joke. It's my name. Indigo
         Clarke.

                    CHESIL
         Really? Wow. What's it mean?

                    INDIGO
         It's a color.

                    CHESIL
         Yeah, but what does it MEAN?

                    INDIGO
         Colors don't have meanings. At least
         nothing definite.

                    CHESIL
         No... Red, that means love.

                    INDIGO
         And anger.

                    CHESIL
         Okay, then Black. That can be
         mysterious.

                    INDIGO
         Or death. Besides, Black isn't a color,
         it's the absence of light. Which makes
         "death" more accurate than--

                    CHESIL
          You're enjoying this, aren't you?

                    INDIGO
          Being right? Maybe.

A soft wind glides across. Chesil shivers. Indigo takes off
his jacket, and puts it around her. She's impressed.

                    INDIGO
          Colors-- actual colors-- have
          different meanings. The one color that
          doesn't? Indigo.

                    CHESIL
          Alright, then. We'll give it one.

She takes a sip of his drink without asking.

                    INDIGO
          ...By all means.

                    CHESIL
          It's a kinda dark Blue, right? Not
          exactly Purple. What's Blue mean?

                    INDIGO
          Sad, depressed--

                    CHESIL
          I was gonna say cool--

                    INDIGO
          --down in the dumps.

                    CHESIL
          --maybe fresh, but hey, we'll go your
          way, Debbie Downer. So, if Indigo is a
          darker Blue...

                    INDIGO
          What's darker than depressed?

                    CHESIL
          Pained. Wounded...

She takes a look at Indigo's pill bottle.

> CHESIL
> ...you've got a broken heart, Indy.
> "Cardilexortol". Sounds heavy.

He gently takes it out of her hands. Puts it away without
eye contact.

> INDIGO
> It's... just over-the-counter.

She sees it's not a subject to discuss. He blows onto his
cold hands. Rubs them.

> CHESIL
> There really is a difference, by the
> way.

> INDIGO
> What?

> CHESIL
> Between knowing and finding out.

> INDIGO
> Oh, yeah?

> CHESIL
> Mm-hm. To know is... well, it's to KNOW.
> Head knowledge, that sorta thing. But
> to find out...

She takes his cold hands. Puts them in the pocket of the
jacket she now wears. They stand mere inches apart.

> CHESIL
> ...that's to learn firsthand.
> Experience.

Indigo smiles. A pretty good breakdown.

> CHESIL
> Not too shabby, huh?

                    INDIGO
          At best? Passable.

                    CHESIL
          Passable??

She playfully hits him. Knocking his drink over the wall.
As they look down in shock:

                    INDIGO
          Tipsy, huh? That a nickname, or on your
          license?

                    CHESIL
          More of a nasty habit, really.

They hear it finally SHATTER. Someone below CALLS OUT in
anger. They back away from the wall. Take a seat on either
side of the tabletop fireplace. In the darkness of the
night, the fire soft-shoes against their faces.

                    CHESIL
          Chesil. Chesil Amoureux.

                    INDIGO
          Marquee name.

                    CHESIL
          It is, isn't it? Partially why I sing.

                    INDIGO
          Professionally?

                    CHESIL
          Getting there. But, don't remind
          anyone. They'll ask me to sing
          something.

                    INDIGO
          Yeah, but you'd love that, wouldn't you?

                    CHESIL
                (dramatic gasp)
          At a funeral? Never!

Indigo cuts her a playful look. Chesil pinches her thumb and index, as if to say: "Maybe just a little bit". They laugh.

                    INDIGO
          "Amoureux". French, right? Something
          about love?

                    CHESIL
          "Lover" to be exact. Well, not exact.
          Could also be "in love". Noun or
          adjective.

                    INDIGO
          And "Chesil"?

                    CHESIL
          Hebrew.

                    INDIGO
          Odd mix.

                    CHESIL
          We are the world.

                    INDIGO
          What's it mean?

                    CHESIL
          Michael Jackson, Quincy Jones...

                    INDIGO
          No, you clown. What's "Chesil" mean?

Beat. She smiles. A soft, beautiful defense mechanism.
Holding back a truth.

                    CHESIL
          You... you don't wanna know.

He looks at her. Truly looks at her. Sees something he
hasn't in a while.

                    INDIGO
          ...Maybe I could find out.

They sit there. Taking in the sight of each other in the flickering light, as we...

DISSOLVE TO

INT. APARTMENT- LIVING ROOM- NIGHT (FLASHBACK)

A WIDOW gently ushers Chesil to the center of the room.

                    WIDOW
          Just one song. Please?

                    CHESIL
          Oh, no... I couldn't--
                    (almost immediately)
          Okay, just one.

Everyone looks on expectantly. Chesil searches the crowd for Indigo. She gives him a wink. Despite her protests, she enjoys singing, no matter the occasion.

A fellow MOURNER grabs a guitar leaning on the wall. Strums an intro. And Chesil sings.

                    CHESIL
          When I first saw your face
          I knew you didn't have a trace
          Of any feelings for me

          And even though I knew your type
          I laughed and built the hype
          You'd walk the ceiling with me

Indigo stands in the doorway. A few people in front of him. Inconspicuous.

                    CHESIL
          Then on the night, before I left
          I swore my lips to never say the truth
          they knew

But, she sees him. And sings through the crowd. Directly to him. Only for him.

18

                    CHESIL
          And then my heart took over me
          And said those simple, foolish words:
          "I love you"

          And the fool thing felt so proud
          Right as it soared above the clouds
          With hopes that you would, too

          And when it saw it was alone
          It fell like stone
          Said nothing, till we said "adieu"

Miraculously, everyone in attendance FADES AWAY: leaving
only Indigo and Chesil. Lit by the surrounding candles
and nothing else.

                    CHESIL
          The months I spent away
          I had to cash in every day
          To buy a different heart

          So when I came back home
          Despite my feeling alone
          I'd have a brand new start

          I see your face
          From underneath my mask
          I'd kill to ask
          Do you remember, too?

          Of when my heart took over me
          And said those simple, foolish words:
          "I love you"

The guitar TAKES OVER. Strumming us through the
memories, as we...

                                        DISSOLVE TO

INT. GREEZY SPOON DINER- NIGHT (FLASHBACK)

Late at night. No one around except the WAITER, and

Indigo and Chesil. They laugh and talk over coffee.

INT. PARK- DAY (FLASHBACK)

Indigo looks on as Chesil frolics through the fallen
leaves. Jumping. Laughing. Like a child.

INT. THE JOINT- DAY (FLASHBACK)

Indigo sits at the bar. Chesil auditions onstage. Ricky
sits front and center.

He eyes her. Wants her. But, Chesil's performance is solely
for Indigo. And he knows it.

INT. THE JOINT- BACKSTAGE- DAY (FLASHBACK)

Ricky makes a move on Chesil. She rebuffs him. Not
interested. He holds up a CONTRACT for her. Wants a kiss
first.

She contemplates. Through the curtains, she sees Indigo
waiting for her by the bar. With a sigh, she takes the
contract.

Rips it.

EXT. STREETS- NIGHT (FLASHBACK)

Pouring rain. The shared umbrella is barely enough. A car
races past, splashing them. Chesil's purse drops. Indigo
bends down to pick it up. Decides now is the time.

From his pocket, he pulls out THE RING: Cheap. Dime a
dozen. Priceless.

                    CHESIL (V.O.)
          I see your face
          From underneath my mask

>   I'd kill to ask
>   Do you remember, too?

She falls to her knees. Hugging him. Kissing him. An obvious answer. Both on their knees, Indigo slips the ring on her finger. Excited for the future, despite the rain.

INT. INDIGO'S APARTMENT- LIVING ROOM- DAY (FLASHBACK)

Indigo puts his arms around her waist. They look at the bottle of Pinot Noir as if it's their child. Their future.

>   CHESIL (V.O.)
>   Of when my heart took over me
>   And said those simple, foolish words:
>   "I love you"

INT. CITY MORGUE- NIGHT (FLASHBACK)

Indigo. Dark coat, dark shirt, dark pants. Almost matching his skin. Cold, empty eyes. Hands in pockets. Beside him, is García. They look down at something. At US.

>   CHESIL (V.O.)
>   I love you...

Indigo just barely nods. García motions to someone off-screen...

>   CHESIL (V.O.)
>   I love you...

...and a WHITE SHEET is laid over us. Taking us to BLACK.

INT. JENNY DIVER'S APARTMENT BUILDING- STAIRWAY- DAY

PRESENT TIME. García walks up, two coffees in hand. THREE UNIFORMED COPS stand talking right outside an apartment. "POLICE-DO NOT CROSS" tape blocking the doorframe.

                    GARCÍA
            Who's first on scene?

                    RIZZOTTI
            That'd be me, ma'am.

She hands him one of the coffees.

                    GARCÍA
            Admission ticket.

                    RIZZOTTI
            Step right up.

He lifts the do-not-cross tape. García ducks under,
entering.

INT. JENNY DIVER'S APARTMENT- LIVING ROOM- DAY

García stands before her CRIME SCENE: Furniture flipped
over. Glass shattered. Blood spilled. And JENNY DIVER's
body.

                    RIZZOTTI
            If I knew I was having company, I'd've
            cleaned up.

García hands him her coffee. Takes out her notepad.
Carefully circles the scene.

                    GARCÍA
            Ever take the test?

                    RIZZOTTI
            For the shield? Been studying.

                    GARCÍA
            Tell me what you see.

                    RIZZOTTI
          Okay... Thirty-one year old victim.
          Female. Living room shows obvious
          signs of--

                    GARCÍA
          Did you know the average time for
          birth labor is eight hours? Two of
          which are spent actually pushing? Out
          of the entire female population, not a
          single woman goes through all that,
          looks her newborn in the eyes, and
          comes up with the name Thirty One Year
          Old Female Victim.

                    RIZZOTTI
          Book says not to get attached.

                    GARCÍA
          Book also says Homicide Division. Book
          says we speak for the dead. Speak up,
          son.

                    RIZZOTTI
          Yes, ma'am. Jennifer Diver, lounge
          singer over at the Razzmatazz--

                    GARCÍA
          Attaboy.

                    RIZZOTTI
          --living room shows obvious signs of a
          struggle, but no signs of forced entry.
          Ms. Diver knew her attacker, or at the
          very least, was familiar with him.

García eyes Jenny's short dress.

                    GARCÍA
          And if she WASN'T familiar, it wasn't
          for a lack of trying.

                    RIZZOTTI
With the amount of blood, it's safe to
say those knife wounds are C.O.D. And
since no one beats up a corpse, it's
even safer to say the beating came
first.

                    GARCÍA
Good so far...

                    RIZZOTTI
Probably best to check the blood, see if
it's all the same type. Perps tend to cut
themselves when using a knife, maybe
ours left us a present. She opened the
door for him, but HE had to close it
when he left, so dust the door for
prints. Also, dust the bottle, since no
man alive lets a woman open it for him,
and dust the bathroom sink and faucet
just in case he washed his hands.
Bleeding victims tend to make things...
well, bloody.

                    GARCÍA
Very good, "detective".

                    RIZZOTTI
In due time, ma'am.

                    GARCÍA
Patiently, I wait. I know you called
C.S.U., call 'em again. I'd rather not
stay here all...

                    RIZZOTTI
...Ma'am?

                    GARCÍA
"Dust the bottle"? What bottle?

                    RIZZOTTI
Right there. Corner.

García carefully makes her way over to the corner.
Avoiding any blood. Kneels down for a closer look.

                    GARCÍA
                   (sighs)
          Of course. Why WOULDN'T it be?

A bottle of wine. Half empty. PINOT NOIR.

INT. INDIGO'S APARTMENT— LIVING ROOM— DAY

Indigo pops awake. Reaches for the floor with urgency.
Fumbles past a half-finished bottle of Jack. A completely
finished bottle of Jack. Grabs a small pot.

He throws up in it. Barely making it.

Indigo sits slumped on the couch. In the same dark coat,
shirt and pants. He's slept in it. Sits frozen. No incentive
to move. Nothing to live for. Something crosses his mind.
He goes for his breast pocket...

...and pulls out the Red Envelope. Stares at it. A cocktail
of fear and regret. Heads for the liquor cabinet. Opens it
to reveal a STACK OF RED ENVELOPES addressed to him. All
unopened. He starts to put the Envelope inside...

...decides against it. Can't let go just yet. Puts the Red
Envelope back in his breast pocket. Heads out the door.

INT. PRECINCT— LOBBY— DAY

Indigo sits on the bench. Staring off into nothingness.
The surrounding noise of CHATTER, YELLING, and RINGING
PHONES don't bother him much.

                    RIZZOTTI (O.S.)
          Sir.

Indigo looks up to see Rizzotti standing before him.

                    RIZZOTTI
          You said you were here to see Detective
          García? Right this way.

Indigo gets up and walks with him.

INT. PRECINCT— BULLPEN— DAY

Rizzotti leads Indigo through. The noise, much louder.
Multiple VOICES overlapping.

                    VOICE 1
          I had NOTHNG to do with that!

                    VOICE 2
          What part of "RIGHT TO REMAIN SILENT"
          do you NOT understand?!

                    VOICE 3
          I wasn't trynna buy "weed", bro! I met
          him in the parking lot to buy "tea"!
          "TEA"!

TWO COPS struggle to handle a MASSIVE PERP. Heading for
Rizzotti and Indigo.

                    MASSIVE PERP
          YEAH, THAT'S RIGHT! BEST BELIEVE I
          SHOT 'IM! TAKE 'IM TO THE HOSPITAL,
          PATCH 'IM UP— I'LL SHOOT 'IM AGAIN!

He bumps into Indigo as he passes. Hard.

                    MASSIVE PERP
          YO, WATCH WHERE YOU GOIN', 'FORE I HAVE
          TO—

The LOOK Indigo gives him, shuts him up quick. Tail
between his legs. Indigo walks off after Rizzotti. Hands
in pockets. One of the cops can't believe it. A mouse just
told an elephant to stick its trunk where the sun don't
shine.

Massive Perp catches the Cop's quizzical look.

                    MASSIVE PERP
          WHATCHU YOU LOOKIN' AT?

INT. PRECINCT- GARCÍA'S OFFICE- DAY

Rizzotti lets Indigo in.

                    RIZZOTTI
          She's with the captain right now. Have
          a seat, I'll let her know you're here.

Indigo sits. His back to the door and Rizzotti.

                    RIZZOTTI
          Want some joe? Water?

Indigo doesn't move. Doesn't speak. Rizzotti shrugs.
Closes the door as he leaves. Muffling the noise from the
bullpen.

Indigo remains in his own thoughts. Sits entirely still.
Until he notices the FILE FOLDERS on García's desk. He
glances down. Looks at the tab on the thickest file.

"MACK THE KNIFE"

The glare in his eye: He recognizes the name.

INT. PRECINCT- BULLPEN- DAY

García exits the captain's office, just as Rizzotti passes
by.

                    GARCÍA
          You got a minute? Need you to make a
          stop for me.

                    RIZZOTTI
          Sure thing. Oh, you got a visitor in
          your office.

                    GARCÍA
          Visitor?

                    RIZZOTTI
          Dark guy. Thin. You had him identify
          that body couple days back. Indigo.

                    GARCÍA
          He's in my office?

                    RIZZOTTI
          Yeah, I put him--

                    GARCÍA
          ALONE?

She hurries off.

INT. PRECINCT- GARCÍA'S OFFICE- DAY

García enters to see her file folders spread all over the
desk and floor. A few posted to the wall. Crime scene
photos, handwritten notes, documents, analysis. The whole
nine.

THE PHOTOS: Women, all young and beautiful. BLOODIED
flooring. Measurements of KNIFE WOUNDS. Bottles of PINOT
NOIR. In the middle of all this...

...is Indigo. Reading the "Mack the Knife" file. He doesn't
look up from it. García is taken aback. Needs a moment to
figure out what to say. Comes up with:

                    GARCÍA
          Sir. I'm gonna have to ask you to leave.

                    INDIGO
          Did he do it?

                    GARCÍA
          I understand you're going through
          something, right now, but I can't have
          you--

                        28

He cuts her a look. Not backing down.

                    INDIGO
          Did. He. Do it?

They stare each other down. García holds her own well
enough, but eventually:

                    GARCÍA
          ...The crime scenes match in every area,
          except one. The victims are all lounge
          singers, beaten in their own home. No
          signs of forced entry, suggesting some
          prior relationship with the killer.
          And there's also the--

Indigo holds up a photo of a bottle of Pinot Noir.

                    GARCÍA
          Yes. There's that. A body was found
          today, which very strongly looks to be
          connected to the many other bodies
          dating back three years.
                    (beat)
          He's back.

Indigo drops the file. Heads for the door, hands in
pockets. García stops him.

                    GARCÍA
          But, where Chesil's crime scene DOESN'T
          match... everyone was knifed. Not her.
          With a name like "Mack the Knife", it's
          not an element he'd suddenly forget.

Indigo heads back for the desk. Pulls a sheet from Chesil's
file.

                    INDIGO
          The eyewitness.

                    CHESIL
          No one alive has seen Mack's face--
          whoever the eyewitness saw running

out of Chesil's building, we have no
OTHER descriptions from the previous
cases to compare it to.

                    INDIGO
          No. The car alarm. She was out shutting
          off her alarm. Could that have scared
          him away?

It's unsettling hearing Indigo use full sentences.

                    INDIGO
          Is it possible he killed her?

                    GARCÍA
          I've given you more than I should've.
          I'm not answering this.

                    INDIGO
          Is it POSSIBLE he was scared off? Ran
          before he could...

He can't finish. Tears threaten to choke his words. THIS is
why he doesn't speak.

His eyes beg the question. Pleading. García holds her own.
Refusing to answer. Indigo storms for the door, brushing
past her.

                    GARCÍA
          INDIGO.

He stops. Doesn't turn back to look at her.

                    GARCÍA
          Don't. This guy... he's been good at this
          game long before he stepped on the
          field. We have nothing on him-- no
          prints, no D.N.A. Today makes eighteen.
          Eighteen souls beaten and knifed, and
          we have nothing to show for it-- I have
          nothing to show for it. Mack was never
          the hobbyist, and has long since
          graduated past expert-- he is

Basquiat. I can't say for sure if he's
responsible for Chesil, but I CAN say
he's dangerous. That is one dog, if you
kick, he will BITE. Stay OUT OF THIS,
Indigo.

Indigo considers. Seriously considers.

                    GARCÍA
        ...Pleas--

The door closes before her word can finish. And Indigo is
gone.

EXT. THE JOINT- NIGHT

Another night. PATRONS are lined up once more to get in.
Moe, Larry, and Curly stand guard.

INT. THE JOINT- NIGHT

JADE reclines atop the grand piano. Ricky fingers the
keys. A tit-for-tat duet. The AUDIENCE eats it up.

They end with a flourish. Standing ovation. Ricky throws
his hand out to Jade, letting the spotlight wash over her.
She savors this moment.

INT. THE JOINT- BACKSTAGE- NIGHT

LATER. Jade has changed out of her dress. In streetwear. As
she packs up her bag to leave, Ricky enters.

                    RICKY
        Pretty good out there.

                    JADE
        Ah. Generous with the compliments, I
        see.

                    RICKY
          Credit where credit's due. Your solos
          are one thing, but when we duet...
          something about the way we duet, can't
          exactly put my finger on it...

Jade sees where this is going. A mile away.

                    JADE
          Chemistry?

                    RICKY
          Is THAT the word I'm looking for?

                    JADE
          Mm-hm. Good night, Ricky.

She walks out with a smile. Ricky calls out after her:

                    RICKY
          Just saying, if you wanna give this so-
          called "chemistry" thing a shot...

                    JADE
          I'll be sure to let you know.

EXT. THE JOINT- BACK ALLEY- NIGHT

Jade exits to a group of FANS. Photos are taken. Autograph
books pushed at her. She takes it in stride: posing and
signing. As she does so--

--she looks off into the distance. A creeping feeling
someone's watching. Brushes it off. Keeps on going.

EXT. STREETS- NIGHT

Jade walks on her way. Softly singing to herself.

REVERSE ANGLE: We see the back of Jade as she walks.
Slowly, we EASE IN on her. Following her. FOOTSTEPS other
than hers are heard.

Jade stops. We stop. The FOOTSTEPS stop. There goes that creeping feeling again.

She walks on. We EASE IN. The FOOTSTEPS continue.

EXT. ELEVATED TRAIN STATION- NIGHT

Jade hurries up the stairs. The TRAIN pulls off. Just missed it. She checks her watch. Waits.

And waits.

Another train GRUMBLES in the distance. Growing. As Jade sings to herself... A SHADOW washes over her back.

> SHADOW (O.S.)
> Pretty set of pipes you got there.

Startled, Jade looks back to see. We don't see his face, though she does. She buries her fear.

> JADE
> ...Thank you.

The train grumbles LOUDER. Closer. Jade turns back around. A polite "Get away from me". The SHADOW is still draped over her.

> SHADOW (O.S.)
> What say you sing a couple songs for
> ME?

The train grumbles LOUDER.

The SHADOW moves in closer.

Jade whips around in cold fear, as a HAND grabs her by the arm, and--

THE TRAIN ROARS PAST as Indigo, from out of nowhere, flips the SHADOWED ASSAILANT over his back. The sounds of struggle are muffled by the ROARING train.

The Assailant gets the best of Indigo. Manages to get back on his feet. Uses his size to his advantage. Grabs Indigo by the collar and inches him closer to the moving train.

Indigo struggles to keep his feet planted. Weight from the Assailant pushes him closer to the edge. Just before he runs out of platform--

--Indigo buckles the Assailant's arms at the elbow and sidesteps. The Assailant loses control of his weight and lunges forward INTO THE SIDE OF THE STILL MOVING TRAIN.

The Assailant spins violently like a top before SLAMMING onto the platform.

Something breaks. Maybe everything.

Indigo locks the Assailant's arm behind his back. Rips through his pockets.

                    INDIGO
          Where's the knife?

                    ASSAILANT
          I don't know what you're--

                    INDIGO
          Where's. The knife?

                    ASSAILANT
          WHAT knife?!

The train disappears into the horizon. Taking rage with it. Breathing heavily, Indigo gets off the Assailant. Lets him limp away. He may be scum... but he's not Mack.

Indigo turns back to look at Jade. She sees the fiery rage in the thin man's eyes. Hurries off, scared.

Indigo stands alone on the platform. Panting.

EXT. THE JOINT- NIGHT

Moe, Larry, and Curly look on as Indio turns the corner.
They ready for round two. Instead, Indigo gets in his car,
parked right across the street.

INT. INDIGO'S CAR- NIGHT

Littered with the signs of a stakeout: food wrappers,
styrofoam coffee cups, water jugs filled with urine.

Indigo spots a SINGER exit The Joint. Eyes her as she
walks on. Sees no one is following her. Waits for his next
opportunity.

                                          DISSOLVE TO

LATER. Still outside The Joint. The night has fallen even
darker. Indigo lifts his glasses, rubbing the bridge of
his nose with thumb and index. Worn out. But, still going.

A KNOCK at the passenger window. He looks over to see
Squid. She gives him a wave. He pays her no mind. She
knocks again. He looks back over. Sees she's holding a
tray of coffee.

chg! He unlocks the door. She gets in.

                    SQUID
          Hi. I take it you remember me? From the
          morgue?

He doesn't answer. Still watching The Joint.

                    SQUID
          Lemme start off by saying that I'm
          sorry. For barging in, for being
          inconsiderate... For your loss.

He doesn't care. She softly laughs to herself.

                    SQUID
          Figured a guy like you don't go for
          condolences. Figured I'd try it out,
          just the same. But, seeing as how you'd
          prefer I cut to the chase, then by all
          means: lemme cut to the chase.

From under her arm, she pulls out a newspaper. Drops it on
the dashboard.

                    SQUID
          I'm a reporter with the Gazette. Well, I
          freelance. Sometimes they buy, most
          times they don't. Was working another
          story at the morgue when I came across
          you.

ANOTHER SINGER exits The Joint. Indigo perks up.
Slightly.

                    SQUID
          Decided to check it out. See if it was
          something worth writing.

A HOODED MAN walks closely behind the Singer. Indigo's
fists tighten on the steering wheel. Waiting for his
moment.

                    SQUID
          Girl like Chesil Amoureux winds up
          dead, first thing I do, I look for the
          ex. Came down to either you, or that
          pretty boy nightingale, Ricky Gordon.

The Singer stops at the corner. Waiting for the light. The
Hooded Man walks closer. Closer.

                    SQUID
          Saw you clamp down on him like a vise
          with lockjaw, so I figure it wasn't you.
          Fact that you let Ricky live...

The Hooded Man turns the corner. Completely passing by
the Singer. Going on his way.

                    SQUID
        ...I figure it ain't him, either.

Indigo calms. Keeps watch, as:

                    INDIGO
        What do you want?

                    SQUID
        Simple answer? YOU.

Finally, he looks at her.

                    SQUID
        I'd say you're not the kinda guy anyone
        would look twice at, but the truth is,
        you're not the kinda guy anyone would
        look at, AT ALL. Beady eyes like a
        hamster, the body of a starving dog,
        not to mention those glasses-- let's
        face it: People should be walking all
        over you. Instead, you square off with
        Ricky's boys, fold them like fresh-
        steamed laundry, and put the fear of
        Yahweh Himself into Ricky, the likes of
        which I have never seen before. I sell
        what I write to the highest bidder, and
        the biddin' ain't so high, 'less what I
        write's got some juice. Guy like you?
        Guy who takes a problem, beats out a
        solution? Guy who hasn't showered or
        changed his clothes since he I.D.'d the
        body? YOU'RE the juice.

She pulls out the coffee from the tray. Offers it.

                    SQUID
        Let's work together. I help you catch
        the-- and I use this term loosely--
        "man" who killed Chesil, the sick freak
        running around playing Cuisinart
        slice-and-dice... And you let me write
        my story with you at the front.

                    37

Indigo considers. Sighs. Takes the olive branch, the
coffee, and--

                    INDIGO
          Get out.

--returns to eyeing The Joint. Squid laughs to herself.
"God, I love this guy".

                    SQUID
          Believe it or not, I figured that, too.
          So, as a show of good faith, I'll give
          you this: You're in the wrong spot.
          Look at the news reports about the
          singers he's knifed, and you'll see that
          Mack doesn't go after girls from big
          clubs like The Joint. He's too smart,
          and this place is too high-profile. He
          goes for holes-in-the-wall like
          Razzmatazz, or even Hotspot where
          Chesil sang after she left Ricky.

Indigo closes his eyes with disappointment. How could he
have missed that? Squid smiles. She loves laying bait.

                    SQUID
          Just a taste of what I know. Call it an
          appetizer. You ever want a meal...

She leaves her card on the dashboard.

                    SQUID
          ...come check out the menu. Coffee's on
          the house.

She exits. Indigo opens his eyes to see the sight of her
walking away. Memories flood in once more. As if she's
right there, he hears her VOICE:

                    CHESIL (V.O.)
          You're killing me, Indy.

                                        CUT TO

INT. INDIGO'S APARTMENT- LIVING ROOM- DAY (FLASHBACK)

Indigo sits on the couch. Chesil stands by the door. Bags in hand. Daytime, but the sun called out sick. Soft rain against the windows. Filling the awkward silence of the room.

                    CHESIL
          ...Please. Say something.

Indigo looks down to the floor. Comatose. She walks over and kneels. Hands on his knees.

                    CHESIL
          It's been my dream. Ever since I was
          four, it was all I've ever wanted to do.
          Singing, traveling, performing... it's
          all I CAN do. And I... I can't do it with
          YOU...

She lifts his head. They stare into each other's eyes. The rain outside stepping in where tears can't. He gives her nothing. Eyes dead to the very sight of her.

She surrenders. Puts her RING on the coffee table. Heads back to the door for her bags.

She stops by the liquor cabinet. Sees their bottle of PINOT NOIR. It's the only bottle there. She touches the glass. Tenderly.

                    CHESIL
          We'll still drink this one day.
          Something simple. Something foolish.

She hoped that would soften the blow. The look Indigo gives her... It does not. He bites his tongue. There ARE words for this, but he refuses to let them loose.

                    CHESIL
          Indy, PLEASE. Say something...

She wants an answer? Fine. He gets up. Takes the Pinot Noir from the cabinet. Forces it into her hands. And right in her ears, he speaks soft, but hard.

                    INDIGO
            I hope it kills you.

He stands there. Drinking in the sight of the blood
rushing from her face. She grabs her bags. Takes her leave
with the bottle.

EXT. INDIGO'S APARTMENT BUILDING- DAY (FLASHBACK)

Chesil exits. Heads across the street... to Ricky. Standing
with an umbrella and an open door to a sleek black car. He
gives her a kiss on the cheek. Before she enters...

...she stops. Feels Indigo standing at the window. We see
him, blurry and distant.She doesn't turn around. With a
sigh, she gets in. Before Ricky does the same, he gives
Indigo a slick smile:

"Got her".

Indigo watches as the car pulls off. Raindrops against the
window like stab wounds on his chest.

INT. INDIGO'S APARTMENT- LIVING ROOM- DAY (FLASHBACK)

Indigo walks off. Loses his step. Grabs his chest. Of
course this would happen now. He pulls his pills from his
pocket. Pops a couple. As he takes a moment to calm...

...he looks at his apartment. At what was once theirs. Now,
barren. Empty.

Lonely.

                                        DISSOLVE TO

EXT. THE JOINT- BACK ALLEY- NIGHT

PRESENT DAY. Ricky exits. Moe and Larry in front. Curly
in back. They walk on their way, but stop when they see
Indigo standing before them.

Moe reaches for his hip, ready to pull, but--

                    RICKY
          Easy, easy...

Indigo walks closer. Under his arm, the newspaper Squid
brought. A ripped out page in his hand. He holds out the
page for Ricky to take. Moe snatches it. Hands it to Ricky
himself. Scribbled on the page:

"RAZZMATAZZ. HOTSPOT. BOGART'S. CLUB 11..."

                    RICKY
          These are dives.

                    INDIGO
          Talk to the bouncers. They see
          anything, they call ME.

                    RICKY
          Anything like what?

Indigo holds out the newspaper for Ricky. Moe goes to
snatch it. Indigo drops it to the ground. If Moe wants to
hand it over so bad, he's gonna have to pick it up. And pick
it up he does. Front page headline:

"LOOK OUT, OL' MACKIE'S BACK!"

                    RICKY
          Jesus...

Indigo turns and walks off.

                    RICKY
          How do you know he did it?

He stops. As matter-of-factly as possible:

41

                    INDIGO
          I'm gonna ask him.

And he walks off into the night.

INT. LOTTE LENYA'S APARTMENT- BEDROOM- NIGHT

LOTTE LENYA hurries in, heading for the closet.

                    LOTTE
          Excuse the mess. Haven't really had a
          chance to clean up. Club's been busy,
          lately. Should be a corkscrew
          somewhere.

She pulls off her clothes. Rummages through the closet. A
flurried search.

                    LOTTE
          I gotta say, you're either really
          fortunate, or really good. I never have
          a nightcap, no matter WHO the guy is.

She pulls out a sexy black dress. Quickly slips it on.

                    LOTTE
          Not that there've been plenty of guys.
          I'm not that kinda girl.

She hurries over to the mirror. Fixes her face and hair a
bit. Smiles at the finished product.

                    LOTTE
          Not that kinda girl at all.

She goes for the door. Takes a moment. Calms herself. Then
sashays out...

INT. LOTTE LENYA'S APARTMENT- LIVING ROOM- NIGHT

...to stand before her GUEST. Oxblood suit. Black fedora.
We only see the back of him as he works on a bottle of wine.

                      42

                              LOTTE
                  Oh. You found the corkscrew.

POP!

                                                        CUT TO

MONTAGE:

-Indigo sits in his car. Phone on the dash. Ever vigilant.
His phone rings. He answers.

-A BOUNCER at CLUB 11 on his cell. Talking hush-hush as
he eyes a MAN chatting it up with a SINGER at the bar.

-Indigo drives off into the night.

-The Man and the Singer walk down the street. Like a
tidal wave, Indigo rushes in. Presses the Man against a
parked car. Flips him over to see his face. The Man's so
old, there's mold. Indigo walks off.

-Back in his car. Waiting. His phone rings.

-ANOTHER BOUNCER. This time at the MOON ROCK A GO-GO.
ANOTHER SINGER chats it up with SOMEONE ELSE.

-Like a hammer, Indigo slams down on him in the middle of
the street. Drags him across the street into the light.
Can't be older than 18. He storms off.

-Again and again: He waits. His cell rings. He moves in.
Each and every tip turns out to be anything but. And each
and every tip etches harder and deeper into Indigo's face.
He sits there, just the same. Still wearing the same dark
coat, shirt and pants. Tired. Worn. Pained. Wounded.

Vigilant.

Maybe even obsessed.

INT. LOTTE LENYA'S APARTMENT- LIVING ROOM- DAY

The CORONER wheels out a BODY BAG. García paces carefully
in the middle of the now-DISHEVELED apartment. Avoids
the blood stains. Kneels down to take a look at the bottle
of PINOT NOIR.

Squid appears in the doorway. Without so much as looking,
García knows she's there.

                    GARCÍA
          This isn't the time.

                    SQUID
          Is it ever? We don't talk like we used
          to.

                    GARCÍA
          We never "talked" AT ALL. You poked,
          and prodded, and connived your way to
          a story, or even worse-- a QUOTE.

                    SQUID
          Ah, but if you took the time to sit and
          talk with me, I wouldn't have to--

                    GARCÍA
          What do you want?

                    SQUID
          Chesil Amoureux. Her ex, the guy who
          I.D.'d her for you.

                    GARCÍA
          He didn't do it.

                    SQUID
          Oh, that I know. What I DON'T know, is
          who he is.

                    GARCÍA
          Said it yourself. He's the ex.

                    SQUID
You and I both know he's so much more.
          (then)
He thinks ol' Mackie killed his girl.

                    GARCÍA
We don't know for sure.

                    SQUID
Yeah... but it's not ENTIRELY
impossible.

Beat. García can read Squid like a book.

                    GARCÍA
You have done some low things, Squid.
So many low things I'm pretty sure even
God's forgotten a thing or ten. But
THIS...?

                    SQUID
Just looking to see who he is.

                    GARCÍA
With no substantiating evidence, you
are validating a broken man's
obsession. All for some story.

                    SQUID
Chesil's a singer. She was beaten. And
she had the bottle of wine. That's
substantiating evidence enough.

                    GARCÍA
THERE WERE. NO. KNIFE WOUNDS.

                    SQUID
Maybe he didn't get the chance. Maybe
he had to go before things got hot. And
maybe... just maybe joe schmoe Indigo
Clarke, as broken and obsessed as he
is... maybe he's the one who finally
takes down Mack the Knife.

45

Squid walks off. She doesn't get too far, before:

                    GARCÍA
          Sydney. The man wants one thing. And at
          the end of the day, you are dangling it
          in front of him, making him carriage
          you to a paycheck.

                    SQUID
          Rachel. We won't know if Mack's
          involved until he's brought in. If
          ANYONE can do that... my money's on
          Indigo. And at the end of that same day
          you mentioned... have you SEEN that
          paycheck?

Squid walks off with a smile.

INT. INDIGO'S CAR- NIGHT

Indigo sits behind the wheel. Stones have more movement
than him. His eyes are bloodshot. Sleep has become a
mythical fantasy.

He waits. And waits. And waits. Finally, his cell rings.

The war rages on.

INT. BOGART'S- NIGHT

Indigo enters the dive of a club. Hands in pockets. Spots
the BOUNCER by the phone. The Bouncer walks over, and:

                    BOUNCER
          I.D.?

Indigo raises a brow.

                    BOUNCER
          No exceptions, buddy. We cardin'
          everyone tonight.

Indigo holds his stare, until:

> BOUNCER
> (whispers)
> C'mon, man. Make it look good...

Indigo plays along. Takes out his license. As the Bouncer scans it:

> BOUNCER
> Far end of the bar. Red, brown, or some kinda suit. Chattin' it up with Ms. Tawdry.

Indigo looks over and sees SOOKIE TAWDRY laughing and boozing with a MAN. Indigo can't make out his face. But with every tip before having been wrong...

He takes his license back and walks off. The Bouncer grabs his shoulder.

> BOUNCER
> Hey, man, this only cuz Ricky Gordon asked a favor. If I'mma take a risk snitchin', you better take a risk and follow through. Now, I look at every guy that comes in here, and nine outta ten of 'em are just mild-mannered creeps lookin' to trip the light fantastic. But this guy... THIS guy? He ain't right. He AIN'T right.

Indigo looks again at Sookie Tawdry and the Man. Still unable to see his face.

INT. INDIGO'S CAR- NIGHT

Indigo gets back in. Takes a moment to think. Looks at his reflection in the side-view mirror. His tired, bloodshot eyes.

He hears her VOICE again:

                    CHESIL (V.O.)
          What is it about death that brings us
          together?

                                                  CUT TO

EXT. CEMETERY– DAY (FLASHBACK)

Indigo turns to see Chesil walking towards him. Both
dressed in black. Surrounded by MOURNERS making their
way to the gravesite.

                    CHESIL
          Two weddings and a baby shower since
          we last saw each other. You weren't
          there for any of them. But this...

                    INDIGO
          Yeah, well... "fun" in funeral, and all
          that.

She softly laughs. He doesn't.

                    CHESIL
          How've you been?

                    INDIGO
          What do you want?

                    CHESIL
          Just... just asking how've you––

                    INDIGO
          Amazing. Excuse me.

He brushes clean past her. On his way for a seat, when––

                    CHESIL
          The ring you gave me had to be the
          cheapest piece of jewelry I'd ever seen.

He stops in his tracks. His back still to her.

                    CHESIL
        They spoil me, you know. Fans,
        managers, agents... Ricky. They see a
        ring, or a necklace, or even a
        diamond-- not attached to anything,
        just a diamond by itself... and they
        give it to me. They all say it's a gift,
        but we all know it's a barter. So many
        sparkling, dancing jewels. All of them
        beautiful beyond my wildest
        imaginations.

                    INDIGO
        You always DID want the best.

                    CHESIL
        I took off your ring. Almost two years
        since, and I can't bring myself to put
        another one on.

He didn't expect to hear that. Still can't bring himself to
turn and look at her.

                    CHESIL
        Nothing compares to that ring. That
        cheap... priceless ring...

He's stunned. It takes a moment. Finally, he does what he
can. He walks away. Leaving her alone with nostalgia.

                                        DISSOLVE TO

LATER. The service goes on. Indigo sits in the back. While
everyone pays attention to the occasion at hand, Indigo
can't take his eyes off Chesil. Sitting a few rows ahead.

He tries to focus. Tries to look away. It doesn't last for
long. He surrenders to her presence. Ashamed of himself
for it.

LATER. The service has finished. Chesil rises from her
seat to leave. Turns behind her to look at Indigo. Sees
only his empty seat. He's already left.

Dejected, she walks on. Makes her way for the exit, when--

                    INDIGO (O.S.)
          Wanna go somewhere?

She turns. Sees that he's waited for her. She smiles
cautiously. Walks off with him.

INT. GREEZY SPOON DINER- DAY (FLASHBACK)

They sit in a booth. Both with coffee.

                    CHESIL
          Is it bad that the whole time I was
          sitting there, I couldn't stop thinking
          it was the boringest funeral I'd ever
          been to?

                    INDIGO
          Pretty sure it's "most boring", and
          yes... yes, that's bad.

She laughs. Her elbow shifts her clutch on the table. A
small, blue BAGGIE slides out. Empty. She puts it back in,
like it was nothing. Effortlessly moves on.

                    CHESIL
          How's the heart treating you?

Indigo clocked all of that. Brushes the thought aside.

                    INDIGO
          Still ticking.

                    CHESIL
          What's the pill again? Car... cardi...

                    INDIGO
          Cardilexortol. Good to know you're
          still tipsy.

                    CHESIL
                (laughing)
        I am not! It's not my fault you don't
        wanna buy heart medicine that
        ACTUALLY SAYS "Heart Medicine" on the
        bottle.

                    INDIGO
        Tell you what: Break me off a piece of
        whatever you make singing, I'll go and
        buy a different heart.

They laugh. As if the past never happened. She smiles at a
realization.

                    CHESIL
        Kinda quoted our song there. "The
        months I spent away, I had to cash in
        every day to buy a different heart"... "I
        see your face, from underneath my mask,
        I'd kill to ask do you remember, too?"

                    INDIGO
        ..."Of when my heart took over me, and
        said those simple, foolish words: 'I
        love you'"

Reciting it brings up so much pain for him. Chesil tries
to soothe it. Involuntarily rubs her nose with a sniff.

                    CHESIL
        Not too shabby, as love songs go.
        Passable, at best.

He scoffs. Can't believe it.

                    INDIGO
        You WOULD think it's a love song,
        wouldn't you? It's got those three
        words in it, so OF COURSE it's a love
        song.

                    CHESIL
        How isn't it?

                    INDIGO
          How could it? It's about a guy who's
          life would've been different if he
          never told her. If he never said those
          simple, foolish words.

                    CHESIL
          Is that so bad? But, then again, that's
          you. Worse-case scenario. A piece of
          plastic in my purse, so I'm a junkie.

                    INDIGO
          I never said--

                    CHESIL
          You never have to. Your eyes say more
          than your lips ever have. You're always
          seeing the anger in Red, or the death
          in Black.

                    INDIGO
          And you, the love and the mysterious.
          If you're still wondering why we didn't
          work out... here it is.

Beat. She can't argue with that.

                    CHESIL
          Girl.

                    INDIGO
          What?

                    CHESIL
          You said the song's about a guy who's
          life would've been different if he
          never said "I love you". I say it's about
          a girl.

She rubs her nose again. Indigo recognizes the tell-tale
signs of an addict. Takes a moment.

                    INDIGO
          Chesil. Hebrew for "fool", isn't it?

                         52

She looks at him. As if her secret's been exposed.

                    CHESIL
          When'd you know?

                    INDIGO
          I knew when I looked it up. I FOUND OUT
          the day you walked away.

Regret weighs heavy on her face.

                    INDIGO
          You're the last person I will ever love.
                    (beat)
          For you, somewhere in there is a
          compliment.

They sit there in silence. Sipping their coffee, as we...

                                        DISSOLVE TO

Indigo's face. Eyes closed. Jaw set. Breathing controlled.
Coated in shadow. We don't move from his face.

We hear: keys JINGLING. A door OPENING and CLOSING. TWO
VOICES.

                    FEMALE VOICE (O.S.)
          Here we are.

                    MALE VOICE (O.S.)
          Nice place.

Indigo opens his eyes. From his tired, bloodshot state, we
realize we're back in the PRESENT DAY. Though, thanks to
the shadow that surrounds him, we have no idea where he
is.

                    FEMALE VOICE (O.S.)
          It gets the job done. Please, make
          yourself comfortable.

                        MALE VOICE (O.S.)
          Actually, you have a bathroom I could
          use?

                        FEMALE VOICE (O.S.)
          Do I have a bathroom? No. There's a
          bucket, though.

                        MALE VOICE (O.S.)
          Ha, ha.

                        FEMALE VOICE (O.S.)
          Down the hall, to the right.

FOOTSTEPS near. Indigo grinds his teeth.

Another door OPENS and CLOSES. Much closer to Indigo.

                        FEMALE VOICE (O.S.)
          Nice of you to pick up some wine. What
          kind did you get?

We hear a ZIPPER sliding down. Indigo's breathing grows
heavier. Ragged.

                        MALE VOICE (O.S.)
          RED.

INT. SOOKE TAWDRY'S APARTMENT- BATHROOM- NIGHT

WHAM! Indigo launches out of the bathtub. Ripping off the
shower curtain and covering the MALE with it. SLAMMING
him against the wall.

                        SOOKIE (O.S.)
          Is everything okay??

The Male (whose face we don't see, thanks to the lights
being off) manages to shove Indigo off.

Indigo hits the tub. Falls back in.

The Male goes for his breast pocket.

                              54

Indigo quickly reaches for something. Anything.

From his pocket, the Male pulls out: snkt! A SWITCHBLADE.

Ladies and Gentlemen: MACK THE KNIFE.

Indigo grabs what he can. A heavy tub of shampoo. Lobs it.

BAM! Square in Mack's face. An extra second for Indigo
to--

--launch back out the tub. Tackling Mack to the floor.
They struggle for the blade. Rise back onto their feet. The
6'2 Mack buckles Indigo's knee. Slamming on top of him on
the floor. The blade glistens in what little light they
have.

The knife edges closer to Indigo. Closer...

                    SOOKIE (O.S.)
            What is going ON in there??

CLOSER.

INT. SOOKIE TAWDRY'S APARTMENT- HALLWAY- NIGHT

Sookie heads for the bathroom door, but--

BOOM! Mack comes flying out. Crashing into the wall.
Sookie sees the knife still in his hand.

                    SOOKIE
            Oh, my God...!

Mack lunges at her.

WHAM! Indigo intercepts, ramming into him.

Mack CUTS Indigo across the bicep. Indigo doesn't cry out.
He powers through. Grabs Mack's knife arm, and--

--flips him over his back. Slamming him on the floor.
Drags him down the hall, towards:

INT. SOOKIE TAWDRY'S APARTMENT- KITCHEN- NIGHT

The lights haven't been turned on, yet. We still don't make
out Mack's face. He scrambles to his feet. Grabs the bottle
of PINOT NOIR from the counter, and--

KSSHHH! Wine SPLATTERS. Indigo falls. A CUT above his eye.
Hits the floor hard enough to knock the pills out of his
pocket.

Mack turns back for Sookie. Sees she's already on her cell.

                         SOOKIE
               Yes, third floor apartment! It's MACK
               THE KNIFE!

Mack ROARS. Furious. Flings the remaining piece of the
shattered bottle at Indigo, who ducks just in time. Takes
off running.

Indigo pushes up to his feet. Winces. His arm's cut pretty
bad. Grabs a dish towel and applies pressure. Runs out
after his prey.

INT. SOOKE TAWDRY'S APARTMENT BUILDING- STAIRCASE-
NIGHT

Mack flies down the dark staircase. Slipping his blade in
his pocket. Moments later...

...Indigo comes stumbling down. Hard. Breaths out of
control.

EXT. STREETS- NIGHT

Indigo whips around the corner. Spins. Can't see Mack
anywhere. The cut above his eye BLEEDS. Can't see. Wipes
the blood away. It still trickles down. Just barely...

...he sees a FIGURE running in the distance. Mack? Maybe.

Indigo launches forward. Keeps pressure on his bicep. Disregards the blood in his eye. Throws one foot in front of the other. Running... Running...

Wobbling... Panting... Gasping... He collapses against a parked car. Heart racing.

No. Not this. Not now.

He continues on. What seems like a half-block dash, is only a three-step stumble.

He falls to his knees. Goes for his breast pocket. Tries to get the pills out. The stupid Red Envelope is in the way. Yanks it out. Digs deeper for the pills.

Can't find it.

His breathing shortens. His chest locks.

He passes out.

                                                    FADE OUT

FROM THE DARKNESS, we hear: a lock JIGGLING. Finally, a KLIK! LIGHT pours in as a door opens, revealing Squid. Coated in the shadow of night. She puts away her lock-pick set. Pulls out a small flashlight.

Mum's the word on where she is right now. The beam of her flashlight shows us snippets: table, chair, flooring. Finally, the beam settles on a LIQUOR CABINET, and we know we're in:

INT. INDIGO'S APARTMENT- LIVING ROOM- NIGHT

Squid almost passes the cabinet by, but sees the STACK OF RED ENVELOPES. Intrigued, she takes one.

INT. INDIGO'S APARTMENT-KITCHEN- NIGHT

The burner ignites. The kettle boils. Steam screams out.
Squid holds the sealed envelope over the steam. It pops
open.

She pulls out the letter. Reads. And as if she was right
there, we hear her VOICE:

                    CHESIL (V.O.)
          Dear Indigo. It's been some time since
          the funeral. Since we last spoke.

                                                  CUT TO

INT. CHESIL'S APARTMENT- LIVING ROOM- DAY (FLASHBACK)

Chesil is in a robe, with her tea. She looks out the
window. The sun in her face. The city skyline... beautiful.
The bottle of PINOT NOIR in front of her, still unopened. A
FRAMED PHOTO of her and Indigo.

She writes a LETTER.

                    CHESIL (V.O.)
          You told me I was the only person
          you'll ever love. I've since realized
          the same about you. I've broken up with
          Ricky.

EXT. THE JOINT- BACK ALLEY- NIGHT (FLASHBACK)

Chesil walks out into the rain. Ricky stands in the
doorway, holding his bleeding head in pain.

                    CHESIL (V.O.)
          There was an argument. And a frying
          pan. There's no going back. And I don't
          want to. I'm at a new club now: Hotspot.

INT. HOTSPOT- NIGHT (FLASHBACK)

Chesil belts out a final note. The CROWD rises. Cheers and
applause.

INT. CHESIL'S APARTMENT- LIVING ROOM- NIGHT (FLASHBACK)

Chesil folds up her letter with a TICKET inside. Puts it in
a RED ENVELOPE. Licks it sealed.

                    CHESIL (V.O.)
               Here's a ticket for my next
               performance.

INT. INDIGO'S APARTMENT- LIVING ROOM- DAY (FLASHBACK)

The Red Envelope slides under the door.

                    CHESIL (V.O.)
               I put a ticket in the last letter I sent.
               But when you didn't show...

We don't see Indigo. Just his HAND as the Envelope is
picked up. Put in the liquor cabinet with others. All
unopened.

TIME LAPSE: More and more letters. All from Chesil. All
unopened.

                    CHESIL (V.O.)
               ...I figured the postman must've went
               through it. Helped himself. Hopefully
               this time you get one who's more honest
               about his work. If the ticket DOES come
               through...

INT. HOTSPOT- NIGHT (FLASHBACK)

Chesil softly sings for her AUDIENCE. They're mesmerized.
As she looks out into the crowd... she eyes an empty seat.

                    CHESIL (V.O.)
        ...I hope you can make it. My finale is
        dedicated to you. Nothing special. Just
        something simple.

Her last note ends with a quiver in her voice. The
audience sees it as good performing. Ignorant to the cries
of her broken heart. They cheer.

                    CHESIL (V.O.)
          Something... foolish.

INT. HOTSPOT- BACKSTAGE- NIGHT (FLASHBACK)

Tears in her eyes, Chesil sniffles. Rubs her nose. She
could be crying. But, we see the blue BAGGIE. And we know
the truth.

                    CHESIL (V.O.)
          Wasn't always yours, but now yours
          forever... Chesil Amoureux.

                                        FADE OUT

INT. HOTSPOT- NIGHT (FLASHBACK)

ANOTHER NIGHT. Chesil is at the bar. Looking at her glass
as it's filled with whiskey. The bartender: a young, wide-
eyed, country boy. Tall and strapping. Innocently
handsome. The BLACK EYE and BAND-AID over his nose adds
to his charm. JODY.

Onstage is LENA LaROY: sexy, silky, and succulent. She
directs the STAGEHANDS on how to set up. From her
flailing arms and gyrating hips, we can tell she's got big
things planned.

                    JODY
          Gonna be one heckuva show, right?

Chesil doesn't respond. Throws back her whiskey. Drops it
down for another. Jody pours.

>   JODY
>   Lena LaRoy. Blessed with a body made
>   for late-night cable T.V. Starts with a
>   golden gown, and ends with nothin' on
>   but her heels. On a good night, even
>   THOSE come off.

Chesil tosses the whiskey back. Disgusted.

>   JODY
>   S'okay. Not a fan of hers, neither. I'd
>   say good talent is few and hard to come
>   by... but it really isn't...

He eyes Chesil as she drops the glass back. The look in his
eyes is familiar. Something simple, and foolish.

>   JODY
>   ...if you know where to look.

As he refills:

>   CHESIL
>   What are you? Six? 6'1?

>   JODY
>   6'2.

>   CHESIL
>   And a chest so big, you could twist a
>   bottle cap between them.

He smiles. Bashful. His "golly, gee-willikers" upbringing
never let him get used to compliments. Especially from
women. Especially from Chesil.

>   JODY
>   Momma always fed me right.

>   CHESIL
>   So, why is it just about every time I
>   see you, you've got a new one?

                         JODY
          Huh?

She taps the bridge of her nose. Signaling his band-aid.

                         JODY
          Oh. I make pretty good tips here. Guess
          it wouldn't be right if SOMEONE wasn't
          beatin' me up for it.

                         CHESIL
          Not the kind to fight back?

                         JODY
          Fightin' back ain't the issue, ma'am.

                         CHESIL
          What is?

                         JODY
          Winnin'.

She smiles as she takes her drink.

                         CHESIL
          Tell me about it.

He smiles back. Softly rests his hand on hers. She looks
into his eyes. Feeling a connection. Something that hasn't
been reciprocated in a while. A long while.

She touches his face. Tenderly. And then:

                         CHESIL
          ...I'm with someone.

Jody's heart shatters. Keeps his composure, but the very
astute can see his soul collapsing into itself.

Chesil tosses back her whiskey. Heads for the exit.

EXT. HOTSPOT— NIGHT (FLASHBACK)

As she leaves, Chesil looks on as WORKERS take down the
sign with her name on it:

"CHESIL AMOUREUX! VOICE OF AN ANGEL!"

And replace it with:

"LENA LaROY! KISS FROM THE DEVIL!"

She walks off.

INT. CHESIL'S APARTMENT— LIVING ROOM— NIGHT (FLASHBACK)

Dark and alone. She enters. Taking off her heels,
stripping down to her slip. Indulges in a SNIFF. Sits at
the table with the Pinot Noir. Pulls out another sheet.

                    CHESI (V.O.)
          Dear Indigo...

                                        FADE OUT

INT. HOTSPOT— NIGHT (FLASHBACK)

Chesil belts. The BAND flourishes and ends. The CROWD
claps. Courteously. Limply. A PATRON holds a flyer in his
hand:

"LENA LaROY! SAX, SEX, AND SKIN! 11PM"

He checks his watch. Only 10:15. Rolls his eyes, and sighs.

INT. HOTSPOT— MANAGER'S OFFICE— NIGHT (FLASHBACK)

The HOTSPOT MANAGER hands out money to Chesil and her
band. A sad amount. The band limps out, grumbling. Chesil
follows behind them, but the Manager takes her by the arm.

                              HOTSPOT MANAGER
                    She's KILLING you out there,
                    sweetheart. You wanna compete, you
                    wanna keep the meat on those bones of
                    yours... you gotta take a lesson from
                    her. Give them what they want.

Beat. Chesil smiles. Takes his hand away.

                              CHESIL
                    I can manage.

INT. HOTSPOT- NIGHT (FLASHBACK)

Chesil walks through, heading for the exit. Lena walks
out onstage in her golden gown. Twirling her mink shawl.
She throws the mink out to the crowd of DROOLING MEN.
Playfully hikes up her gown.

Jody is at the bar. A BAND-AID above his right eye, this
time. As Lena teases to show everything, Jody looks at the
one who shows nothing.

He looks at Chesil.

EXT. BANK- DAY (FLASHBACK)

Chesil stands in front. Staring at the sign:

"SAVINGS AND LOANS"

INT. BANK- DAY (FLASHBACK)

The BANKMAN looks on as Chesil contemplates. The DOTTED
LINE is frightening. She takes a breath. And signs her
soul.

INT. VARIOUS CLUBS AND LOUNGES- DAY/NIGHT (FLASHBACK)

CLUB 11. Chesil speaks with the MANAGER. He shows her a

                                64

flyer for Lena LaRoy.

MOON ROCK A GO-GO. The MANAGER shakes his head no.

DANNY BOY'S. As Chesil pitches herself... she sees a sign for Lena being hoisted up.

BOGART'S. Chesil walks in... only to see Lena onstage, directing the set up. Chesil stands frozen.

Lena locks eyes with her. Gives her a wink.

INT. HOTSPOT- NIGHT (FLASHBACK)

Jody, tissues up his bloodied nose, pours Chesil a drink. Coming up behind her, is Ricky.

> RICKY
> Didn't have to leave, you know. People
> break up all the time.

He notices the run in her stockings. Cheap dress on her back.

> RICKY
> Loan ran dry, huh?

He places a CONTRACT on the bar.

> RICKY
> Enough's enough. Come home, little
> birdie. Lemme take care of you.

He rests his hand on her shoulder. No one's touched her in a while. She tosses back her drink. Drops her glass on the contract.

Doesn't even look at it.

EXT. STREETS- DAY (FLASHBACK)

Chesil hurries across the street. The Bankman on her

heels, briefcase in hand.

> BANKMAN
> Ms. Amoureux! Ms. Amoureux, your
> payment is due!

INT. CHESIL'S APARTMENT BUILDING- HALLWAY- NIGHT
(FLASHBACK)

BOOM! BOOM! BOOM! The LANDLORD bangs on the door.
Furious.

> LANDLORD
> This AIN'T a FREE TICKET, kid!

INT. CHESIL'S APARTMENT- LIVING ROOM- NIGHT (FLASHBACK)

Chesil lies out on the floor. Tears streaming. Eyes red.
Could be sorrow. Could be the blue baggie beside her. When
you think about it, aren't they both the same?

> LANDLORD (O.S.)
> You hear me?! You wanna sleep for FREE,
> you sleep on the STREET!

Chesil crawls back to the table. The table with the Red
Envelopes. The table with the Pinot Noir.

She writes.

INT. RAZZMATAZZ- DAY (FLASHBACK)

Chesil. A wreck of a woman. Barely held together by humble
makeup and humble attire. A far cry from how she used to
be. She auditions for the RAZZMATAZZ MANAGER.

> CHESIL
> Sometimes at night I write myself a
> letter
> Just so I can hear your voice
>
> I write to dry my tears

Phrases from over the years
I write to feel your breaths
Press them close to my chest

I make you say that I'm the only one
Read it back and shout with rejoice
Sometimes at night I write myself the
saddest letter
Just so I can hear your voice...

He rises to his feet. Clapping like his life depended on
it.

> RAZZMATAZZ MANAGER
> PERFECT! Perfect, perfect, PERFECT! Ms.
> Amoureux, you are EXACTY what I've
> been looking for.

She can't believe it. Tries to carry on as if she gets this
all the time. She doesn't. She hasn't. He walks onstage.
Shakes her hand vigorously.

> RAZZMATAZZ MANAGER
> How soon can you get ready?

> CHESIL
> How soon do you need me?

> RAZZMATAZZ MANAGER
> Ms. Amoureux, I need you front and
> center tomorrow night, and every
> night following. Your poise, your
> control, your VOICE! I'd say I'd fall in
> love with you if I weren't a married
> man, but I AM a married man, and I'm
> STILL falling in love with you!

Chesil laughs. Even a few tears.

> RAZZMATAZZ MANAGER
> You're gonna need your own band,
> however. And some new clothes.
> Something elegant. Something
> STRIKING.

                    CHESIL
          I... I don't have the money right now
          for--

                    RAZZMATAZZ MANAGER
          Never you mind that, young lady. I can
          advance you the cash to start up and
          take it out of your pay-- in
          reasonable amounts, of course.

                    CHESIL
          Oh, thank you. Thank you so much, sir.

                    RAZZMATAZZ MANAGER
          No, no, my dearest dear...
                    (kisses her cheek)
          ...thank YOU.

INT. RAZZMATAZZ- MANAGER'S OFFICE- DAY (FLASHBACK)

Chesil signs a CONTRACT. The Manager hands her a couple
stacks of cash.

                    RAZZMATAZZ MANAGER
          Blow us away, sweetheart.

INT. CHESIL'S APARTMENT- LIVING ROOM- DAY (FLASHBACK)

Chesil enters. Excited. Prancing and twirling around.
She goes for her blue baggie--

No. Never again. She tosses it in the garbage. A new life.
Better. Brighter.

EXT. STREETS- DAY (FLASHBACK)

Her band is now playing on the corner. She hands them
some money. They shake her hand, eager to get back
together again.

INT. CLOTHING STORE- DAY (FLASHBACK)

Chesil tries on dress after dress after dress. Not sure
which to choose.

INT. CHESIL'S APARTMENT- BEDROOM- DAY (FLASHBACK)

She settles on something simple. Familiar. Drop dead
gorgeous. A white dress.

She looks herself over in the mirror. It's like being in
her old skin again. For once, things are as they should be.

INT. CHESIL'S APARTMENT- LIVING ROOM- NIGHT (FLASHBACK)

Just as before... Chesil writes a letter for Indigo. Puts in
a flyer for Razzmatazz.

INT. RAZZMATAZZ- NIGHT (FLASHBACK)

She enters. White dress under her coat. A pep in her step.
She passes by the BARTENDERS and WAITRESSES, heading
to--

INT. RAZZMATAZZ- BACKSTAGE- NIGHT (FLASHBACK)

She looks through the window of the Manager's office. Sees
the Manager grinning wildly as:

Lena stands before him. Giving him a glimpse of the
performance she's bared for everyone else. With a
handkerchief, the Manager wipes the sweat from his brow.
And shakes Lena's hand.

Chesil is broken. As Lena looks through the window, too.
And smiles.

INT. CHESIL'S APARTMENT BUILDING- HALLWAY- NIGHT
(FLASHBACK)

Chesil storms for her door. The Landlord is already there,
POUNDING. He sees her:

                    LANDLORD
          You want me to break the door down?! I
          don't care! I've got the money for it! I
          KNOW how to pay for things!

INT. CHESIL'S APARTMENT- LIVING ROOM- NIGHT (FLASHBACK)

The door opens. Chesil enters--

                    LANDLORD
          I've got every right! I can take you by
          the ankles and DRAG YOU OUT IN THE--!

--and SLAMS the door in his face. She tries. The poor
thing TRIES to get ahold of herself. Tears streaming down.
Breaths punching out.

She can't. She goes for the garbage. Dumps it out. Searches
through, until she finds... the baggie.

Finds solace.

EXT. STREETS- NIGHT (FLASHBACK)

Lena walks on her way. Drunk. Happy. Heels in hand.
Coming out of the shadows behind her...

...is Chesil. Eyes wired. Spazzing in their sockets. Her
nose, red. Raw. She closes in like a lioness.

For the kill.

                                             CUT TO

INT. HOTSPOT- NIGHT (FLASHBACK)

Another night. Chesil tosses back a whiskey. Drops the glass down. As Jody, BUSTED LIP, refills:

> JODY
> You heard?

> CHESIL
> Yeah.

> JODY
> Lena's out of action.

> CHESIL
> I heard.

> JODY
> Her spot's open now.

> CHESIL
> I know.

> JODY
> You should ask.

> CHESIL
> I did.

> JODY
> What'd they say?

> CHESIL
> Same as they always do.

She tosses back her whiskey, and, with tears in her eyes:

> CHESIL
> "Strip".

Jody feels for her. Truly. As Chesil places the glass back down... he sees her BRUISED KNUCKLES. There's a question on his tongue.

But it never reaches his lips.

INT. HOSPITAL- NIGHT (FLASHBACK)

Lena sits in bed. Completely covered in shadows. A CAR
rolls past outside. Its HEADLIGHTS bleed through the
Venetian blinds...

...revealing her FACE. Her career is over.

We return to the shadow. Another CAR passes outside. We
get another glimpse. Again and again, as Lena stares off
at:

Hotspot. She's got a clear line of sight of the WORKERS
outside. TAKING DOWN HER NAME.

As CARS pass by and HEADLIGHTS bleed in, we see her
painful contemplation. Of jealousy.

Of hate.

INT. CITY MORGUE- HALLWAY- NIGHT (FLASHBACK)

Indigo sits on the steel bench. García stands before him
as he looks at the crime scene photos.

                    CHESIL (V.O.)
          What is it about death that brings us
          together?

                                        DISSOLVE TO

INT. INDIGO'S APARTMENT- LIVING ROOM- NIGHT

PRESENT DAY. Squid is on the floor. Reading Chesil's
letters with her flashlight. A pile of them beside her. All
opened.

Finished, she looks up from the letter. As if coming up for

air:

                    SQUID
          Christ...

EXT. GREEZY SPOON DINER- NIGHT

Late into the night. Through the windows, we see very few
inside. A FIGURE limps towards it.

INT. GREEZY SPOON DINER- NIGHT

Squid sits at the bar. Hears the BELL above the door, and
turns to see:

Indigo. An utter wreck. Still in the same clothes since he
I.D.'d the body. Beyond the state of wrinkled. Sagging.
Through his glasses, we see his eyes have sunken in. The
already thin man has not been eating.

Squid waves him over. It takes a moment. It takes
everything for him to put one foot in front of the other.
This place has meaning for him.

He walks over. Takes a seat at the counter. Squid notes
that on his wrist, is a band from the hospital.

                    SQUID
          How's the ticker?

He doesn't answer.

                    SQUID
          Want coffee? Something stronger? On
          me.

He doesn't look at her.

                    SQUID
          I gave you my card. YOU called ME. You
          still gonna make me work for it?

                    (beat)
You had him. Not the cops, not the feds.
Seven-some-odd BILLION people on the
face of this planet, eight MILLION in
this city alone... and that's more than
any of them could ever say. YOU had
him.

His eyes are open. His heart beating. But, make no mistake:
he's dead.

                    SQUID
I looked into you. No priors, so you're
not with the mob. Nothing classified
or redacted, so you're not military.
The only thing I could find was name,
date of birth, and a brief subscription
to Bird Watcher's Monthly, for reasons
obvious, and yet... not.
                    (then)
Oh, then there's the small mention of
your name and address in a detective's
report about four years back. Murder
case. Victim grew up on the same block
as you. Childhood friend, I'm guessing.
He died, the cops knew who did it, but
couldn't so much as prove the hair on
his butt... when miraculously, like a
gift from the heavens above, Prime
Suspect Number One and Only, a
previously healthy and untouched man,
limps into, of all people, the POLICE
COMMISSIONER's office, wincing in
pain from the broken rib or three,
unequivocally confessing to your
friend's murder. Cops had some
questions for you, but you were
unavailable for comment. Disappeared
off the face of the earth... until now.
Until Chesil.

She moves in closer. Looking at him like a biology
student does a frog.

                    SQUID
          No. No, you're not mob. You're not
          military. You are MAN. Nothing more
          than a man. One who exists under very
          specific circumstances. One who LIVES,
          only when someone DIES.

She rests her hand on his. Selling this.

                    SQUID
          I won't pretend to be noble. I won't
          insult you with a con. I said it before,
          I'll say it again: You're the juice, the
          kick my story needs. But, I can't have
          you screwing my rep. Getting sued is
          sorta like how any rational parent
          views Disneyworld: Been there twice,
          I'd rather not go a third.
                    (then)
          I need your okay. You do that, you give
          me that... and I will give you the last
          clue I've gathered from investigating
          Mack the Knife. The only clue I don't
          think the cops've put together. A clue
          I've been saving for a moment just like
          this.

She's worn him down. And she can smell it. As he nods in
agreement, she smiles.

                    SQUID
          He's not on his own.

A spark of life in Indigo's being. Tiny. But just enough.

                    SQUID
          No leads. A city on edge for THREE
          YEARS. Everyone suspicious of every
          cat in the bush, everyone checking
          behind the curtains in the shower...
          yet he still kills unseen. How?

She whispers in his ear:

                    SQUID
          Protection.

Indigo is close. So close he could taste it. Squid writes
something down on a napkin.

                    SQUID
          Good thing you're not mob. It'd be a
          severe conflict of interest when you
          knock on THIS guy's door.

She slides the napkin to him with a smile.

                    SQUID
          Happy hunting.

Indigo looks at the napkin on the counter. Captain Ahab
holding the heart of Moby Dick.

EXT. STREETS- NIGHT

OZZIE, fat, well-dressed and pompous, exits a building. He
crosses the street. Gets into the backseat of a TOWN CAR.

INT. OZZIE'S CAR- NIGHT

                    OZZIE
          Home.

Nothing.

                    OZZIE
          You ain't hear me? I said--

Indigo, in the driver's seat, turns around.

                    OZZIE
          What the... where's Sy?

                    INDIGO
          Right behind us.

                    OZZIE
          What is this?

                    INDIGO
          You own the muscle in this town.

                    OZZIE
          You some kinda cop?

Indigo throws the car in REVERSE. Speeds backwards to an
intersection. He doesn't look. Doesn't use the rear-view
mirror. 50MPH.

                    OZZIE
          Have you LOST your mind?

                    INDIGO
          You own the muscle in this town.

                    OZZIE
          YES! You GOT IT, okay?! This supposed to
          be some kinda shakedown?

                    INDIGO
          Protection for a price. I need a list of
          customers.

                    OZZIE
               (laughs)
          You're not getting ANYthing outta--

VROWWW! The town car, still reversing, blitzes through
the intersection. Just barely missing an 18-WHEELER.

                    OZZIE
          JEEZUS CHRIST! Pull over!

55MPH. Indigo still doesn't look where he's reversing.
Ozzie tries to get out, but-- chg! The doors lock.

                    INDIGO
          I need a list.

                    OZZIE
        You are dead. You hear me? You gotta
        step outta this car SOMEtime, and when
        you DO, you are--

MUFFLING is heard from the trunk. THUMPING.

                    OZZIE
        What's that?

                    INDIGO
        I told you: Sy's right behind us.

They reverse through another intersection. Kissing a
SEDAN with a KLAP! A love tap. But at 60, now 65MPH...

                    OZZIE
        You're CRAZY! You hear me? PULL OVER!

                    INDIGO
        Two intersections without a scratch.
        We owe death a debt. Soon as we hit that
        third one back there...

Ozzie whips around to see the river-like INTERSECTION.
They will NOT survive this one.

                    INDIGO
        ...we overdraft.

                    OZZIE
        Christ... stop the car, I'll tell you
        what you want.

70MPH.

                    OZZIE
        Stop the car, and I'll--!

75MPH.

                    INDIGO
        ALRIGHT! THE SPRINGS 'N' FEATHERS
        HOTEL!

ERRRRKKKSSSSS! The town car screeches to a stop. Rubber burning. Just barely entering the intersection. Avoiding collision.

                    INDIGO
          What about the Springs 'n' Feathers?

                    OZZIE
          You owe me new pants, you know that?

Indigo cuts Ozzie a look.

                    OZZIE
               Alright. Fine.

INT. SPRINGS 'N' FEATHERS HOTEL— LOBBY— NIGHT

Mack the Knife walks up to the FRONT DESK CLERK. Dressed as usual: Oxblood suit, black fedora, black-and-white wingtips. We still don't see his face.

                    OZZIE (V.O.)
          Runs like any other hotel, more or
          less. 'Cept we got a "special services"
          program for any mug who'd rather not
          use a credit card.

Mack hands the Clerk a wad of cash. The clerk pockets it, and hands him a key card. Mack heads for the elevator and steps on. He turns, facing US. Head down, fedora covering his face. With a SMILE...

                    OZZIE (V.O.)
          For a small, cash-only fee, you get put
          up close to the exits, cop-sniffers left
          and right, and the best room service
          this side of the Mississippi. The kind
          where everyone keeps their eyes
          closed, and their mouths shut.

...the elevator closes.

INT. OZZIE'S CAR- NIGHT

                    OZZIE
          More you pay, more you get. Mini-Bar,
          hot towels, broads-- you name it. Even
          got armed soldiers making rounds, just
          in case people like YOU get nosy. That
          everything?

                    INDIGO
          A list. Anyone who's paid top price.

                    OZZIE
          Gimme a couple days, and--

Indigo lets off the brake. The car jerks backwards into
the intersection.

                    OZZIE
          Okay, okay! Lemme make a call.

As Ozzie pulls out his cell, Indigo finally uses the rear-
view mirror. But, only to look at himself. He sees his own
mortality. Doesn't care.

INT. THE JOINT- NIGHT

After hours. Indigo sits at the bar. Working on a glass of
whiskey. The BARTENDER pours him drink after drink.
Indigo tosses them all back.

Moe, Larry, and Curly are nearby. Hands on their holstered
guns. Watching Indigo closely.

Indigo drops his glass for another. The Bartender denies
him. Indigo sits there. Staring into the dry glass. Eyes
numb, and wet.

The glass fills up once more. It's Ricky that pours the
shot. Pulls out another glass. Pours one for himself, too.
Not his biggest fan, Indigo looks at him.

                          RICKY
            He took our girl. Make 'im pay.

Indigo pumps the bad blood aside. Gives Ricky a slight
nod.

They drink.

                                          DISSOLVE TO

EXT. SPRINGS 'N' FEATHERS HOTEL- BACK ALLEY- NIGHT

Indigo makes his way over. Still in the same clothes. Dark
coat, shirt, and pants. Hands in pockets.

A GOOMBAH leans on the back entrance. Smoking a
cigarette. Just as he sees Indigo approach from the
shadows--

WHAM! Indigo lays into him. He folds like a chair. Indigo
enters.

INT. SPRINGS 'N' FEATHERS HOTEL- KITCHEN- NIGHT

He makes his way through the busy CHEFS and WAITERS.
Powering through.

A GUNMAN sits at a small table with a plate of lasagna. Gun
sticking out from under his shoulder. Reading the paper:
"MACKIE'S BACK IN TOWN!"

Indigo kicks the chair out from under him. He goes down.
Indigo goes down with him. Whatever he does to him...

The chefs and waiters are too busy to notice.

Indigo drags the unconscious Gunman to the corner.
Stashes him under the tablecloth of a serving cart.

                            81

INT. SPRINGS 'N' FEATHERS HOTEL- CLEANING SERVICES-
NIGHT

Indigo walks through. Grabs a SECURITY BLAZER from a
rack.

INT. SPRINGS 'N' FEATHERS HOTEL- STAIRCASE- NIGHT

He heads up. Three at a time. Takes off his coat. Puts on
the blazer.

INT. SPRINGS 'N' FEATHERS HOTEL- SECURITY HUB- NIGHT

Indigo enters. The FOUR SECURITY GUARDS barely look at
him. All they see is a blazer that matches theirs. "Good
enough". They go back to their conversation. Completely
disregarding the CAMERA FEEDS.

Indigo spots an EXTENSION CORD. Every wire known to man
plugged in. A half-empty COFFEE CUP on the table above it.
He moves the cup back a bit.

Then tips it over.

INT. SPRINGS 'N' FEATHERS HOTEL- ELEVATOR- NIGHT

He steps in and hits a floor button. Replaces the blazer
with his usual coat. Back in business. The door opens on
another floor--

--revealing a LONE GUARD. He spots the blazer in Indigo's
hand. His eyes flash an intuition of suspicion.

Indigo grabs him. Yanks him inside.

INT. SPRINGS 'N' FEATHERS HOTEL- SECURITY HUB- NIGHT

The coffee from the tipped over cup has poured out across
the table. Starts to drip on the overcrowded extension

cord.

INT. SPRINGS 'N' FEATHERS HOTEL- ELEVATOR BANK- NIGHT

Indigo walks out of the elevator. The Lone Guard inside.
On the floor. Unconscious.

INT. SPRINGS 'N' FEATHERS HOTEL- SECURITY HUB- NIGHT

The guards laugh at a joke. One finally glimpses at the
camera feeds. Skipping. Repeating. Fading in and out.

He calls everyone's attention. They spot the sparking and
sizzling extension cord, thanks to the spilled coffee.
Before the feeds die entirely, they just barely make out
one thing:

Indigo.

INT. SPRINGS 'N' FEATHERS HOTEL- STAIRCASE- NIGHT

FIVE GUARDS make their way up. No time to lose.

INT. SPRINGS 'N' FEATHERS HOTEL- PENTHOUSE FLOOR-
NIGHT

Indigo moves through the hall. A shark through water. The
staircase door opens and the five security guards flood
out. They run for him. An attempt to rush him...

INDIGO TAKES HIS HANDS OUT HIS POCKETS.

The combined weight of all five guards equals upwards of
800lbs. Indigo powers through regardless. The harder
they clamp down on him, the faster he breaks free.

What was FIVE, becomes FOUR. What was four, crumbles to
THREE. Three becomes FOUR once more, one determined not
to go down.

Indigo puts him back in his place. And it's one-on-THREE once more.

Three shrinks to TWO. Two inevitably becomes ONE. When all is said and done...

..Indigo is the only one left standing. As he moves for the end of the hall:

His two hands. Out of his pockets. Fingers flexing. Open, then curled. Open, then curled.

INT. SPRINGS 'N' FEATHERS HOTEL- PENTHOUSE- NIGHT

KROOM! The door is KICKED clean off its hinges. Indigo flushes through, like a windstorm.

Searching. Searching.

INT. SPRINGS 'N' FEATHERS HOTEL- PENTHOUSE- BATHROOM-NIGHT

Indigo enters. Mack quickly rises out of the full bathtub, only a quarter-second to make a move...

...he doesn't take it. The way Indigo stands by the door, like a land mass that has always BEEN... Mack knows there is no escape. As he stands, naked and wet:

Indigo stands before him. The same way he did Ricky, once. A lion. Ragged breaths. Peppered with snarls. His anger crowds the room, until--

--he realizes Mack's face. With the lights on, finally he sees everything: Soft skin. Strong chin. Electric brown eyes. A handsome, almost beautiful, man exuding light. Mack smiles.

                    MACK THE KNIFE
          What were you expecting? Satan?

EXT. STREETS– NIGHT (FLASHBACK)

Suddenly, we're slammed back in the PAST. Chesil exits a
dark alleyway. Rubbing her nose. Five steps out and she
sees Jody on the curb: Bloody nose. Swelled cheek. His
THREE ATTACKERS running away, laughing.

> CHESIL
> Oh, my God...! Jody!

She runs over. Kneels down to him.

> CHESIL
> Look what they did to you...

> JODY
> S'okay...

> CHESIL
> (to Attackers)
> Pretty brave when it's three-on-one!

> JODY
> Chesil, it's okay... I'm fine...

> CHESIL
> No, you're not, you're a mess. What
> happened?

> JODY
> Oh, you know... couple guys after my
> tips again. Decided to beat up their
> fists with my face. Tale as old as time.

He tries to smile. His cheek throbs in pain.

> JODY
> Looks like you had a rough night, too.

> CHESIL
> What?

Her hair's matted with sweat. Eyes twitching left and
right. But mostly... her nose bleeds. She quickly wipes it
away.

                    JODY
          Never mind me... are YOU good?

                    CHESIL
          I'm... I'm fine...

                    JODY
          What're you doin' out here anyways?

                    CHESIL
          Nothing, I...

From the same alleyway Chesil came from: TWO MEN step
out. Before they go their separate ways, they "shake
hands"-- transferring a wad of cash and a blue baggie
from palm to palm.

Jody looks at the half-second DRUG DEAL. Then back at the
wired-eye, twitching-nose Chesil.

                    CHESIL
          Was just going for a walk.

She puts her arm around him. Helps him to his feet.

                    CHESIL
          Come on. Let's get you cleaned up.

                    JODY
          Yeah. You and me BOTH.

They walk off into the night.

INT. CHESIL'S APARTMENT BUILDING- HALLWAY- NIGHT
(FLASHBACK)

They walk up to her door. Spot an EVICTION NOTICE. Before
Jody can say a word, she rips it off. Crumples it.

INT. CHESIL'S APARTMENT- LIVING ROOM- NIGHT (FLASHBACK)

They enter. Chesil sits him down on the couch. She goes off into the kitchen. As we hear water RUNNING and cabinets OPENING...

Jody notices the FRAMED PHOTO on the table. Chesil and Indigo. Together. Happy.

Chesil returns with a pot of water and a rag. Kneeling in front of him, she damps the rag and rests it on his cheek.

He winces. She shushes.

Their eye contact never breaks as she cleans his cheek and lips. He falls further and further into her eyes. Two never-ending portals-- wired as they may be.

Higher than the Chrysler, she's still beautiful.

Chesil feels the attraction herself. And gives in. Just a little. Her thumb softly caresses the curve of Jody's chin. Her eyes lock onto his lips. His fingertips slide on her forearm--

--and she pulls away. Remembering her loyalty. Her "committed relationship". She starts to walk off, but Jody rises. Takes her by the arm.

> JODY
> Chesil. That night Ricky stopped by
> Hotspot. The night he offered you
> another contract. He stayed for a
> drink after you left. Then had a couple
> more. He told me 'bout Indigo. 'Bout
> what you two were. What you tried to be
> again. How he turned his back on you,
> same as you once did him.

The mere mention of Indigo's leaving her... a pain reflex on her face. She tries to bury it.

> CHESIL
> Ricky shouldn't have.

                    JODY
          Can't say I'm upset he did. Always knew
          there was a pain in you. A sharp one.
          The kind where you can't breathe too
          deep. So many things in the world
          trynna tear us down, beat us up, and
          leave us on the curb...

He softly turns her to face him.

                    JODY
          ...last thing we need... last thing YOU
          need... is a broken heart.

She doesn't want to look. Doesn't want to give in. He
delicately raises her chin. His thumb rubs her cheek.

                    JODY
          I can be good to you.

                    CHESIL
          I know, Jody, I--

                    JODY
          I WILL be good to you.

                    CHESIL
          It's more than that, Jody. He--

                    JODY
          I won't leave you out in the wind. Not
          like he did. No ma'am.

                    CHESIL
          Jody. You don't know him like I do. He
          trusted me with the one thing he
          prized the most... and I SHATTERED it.
          Threw it away. And despite that, he
          keeps on. He survives.

                    JODY
          Ricky told me all about Indigo and his
          friend that died. He brought a man to

justice, yeah, but that ain't survivin'.
That's livin' for death.

                    CHESIL
          He's more than that...

                    JODY
          He ain't what you need.

                    CHESIL
          Maybe so. But he IS what I WANT.

That hurts. The both of them.

                    CHESIL
          I don't know. Maybe it's guilt. Maybe
          it's nostalgia. Maybe it's a toxic mix
          of both-- me trying to get back to how
          things were. But, that's what I want.
          Everything I lost. I want them BACK.

He softly touches her cheek.

                    JODY
          That ain't guilt. That's just foolish.

She rests her hand on his. Falling into his touch.

                    CHESIL
          ...If only you knew.
               (then)
          You're sweet, Jody. But, Indigo... he
          lets no one knock him down. Not even
          me. After everything I've put him
          through... he's strong.

Jody touches the bruise on his cheek. Hurt inside and out.

                    JODY
          ...Always comes down to that. Don't it?

They stand silent. Unbearably so, as we...

                                        DISSOLVE TO

INT. SPRINGS 'N' FEATHERS HOTEL- PENTHOUSE- BATHROOM-
NIGHT

Indigo stands before Mack, who's still standing in the
tub.

                    INDIGO
          I didn't have any reason to think she'd
          leave me the way she did. Why would I?
          She was everything I'd ever wanted,
          with a splash of everything I didn't
          even know I needed. Loved her. Put that
          ring on her. Saved that bottle with
          her... No. I didn't have ANY reason to
          think she'd leave me.

Indigo backs away. Takes a seat on the toilet cover. Mack's
eyes follow him. Genuinely interested.

                    INDIGO
          Bumped into her again a couple years
          later. And right there-- I swear to
          God, right there... I saw it. Looked in
          that woman's eyes, and despite the fact
          that we looked at the world through
          two different lenses, I SAW the truth.
          And right then, I didn't have any
          reason to think she'd leave me AGAIN.

He fights the tears.

                    INDIGO
          Should've taken her back. The
          loneliness, the drugs... I saw that, too.
          Should've taken her back, just the
          same. But, it's not easy giving someone
          your heart the first time around. A
          SECOND time?

He chuckles. The only joke in his universe, is himself.

                    INDIGO
        I was scared. Nothing scares me. The
        mob, the cops, YOU... nothing. But, her?
        Chesil?
                (then)
        Did you know her first name's Hebrew?
        Means "fool". Her last name, that can go
        two ways. Noun or adjective. Can mean
        "lover", or "in love". So which is it?
        Who was she? The "fool lover"? Or was
        SHE the "fool in love"? I'm scared of
        the answer, too.

He rises. Walks back over to Mack.

                    INDIGO
        Wish I wasn't too scared to try again.
        Too scared to give her a second chance.
        And now...

Fearing Indigo's next move, Mack backs into the corner of
the tub. Trying to get as far away as he can.

                    INDIGO
        ...now it's too late. Far too late to
        realize that the second time around...
        she would've ACTUALLY been good to me.
        Pretty foolish, huh?

Indigo gets into the tub. Standing over his naked,
vulnerable prey. Speaking in a terrifyingly calm tone.

                    INDIGO
        Chesil Amoureux. Before you go, you
        are going to say her name. Chesil.
        Amoureux.

He inches closer. Closer. His shadow casting over Mack,
who can back up no further. Shining through the dark
shadow, is Mack's pearly-white shark-like grin as:

                    MACK THE KNIFE
        Who?

                        91

INT. CHESIL'S APARTMENT- LIVING ROOM- NIGHT (FLASHBACK)

Right where we left them. Jody and Chesil stand silent. Unbearably so. Jody does something he's probably never done before:

He clenches his fist.

                    JODY
          Just 'bout gettin' TIRED of people
          thinkin' I ain't man enough as I SHOULD
          be.

                    CHESIL
          Jody... I wasn't saying--

He backs her into a corner. Using his height as a threat. Seething with offense. Rage.

                    JODY
          Wasn't sayin' what? I'm not strong
          enough? Not strong enough like Indigo
          for you? Lil' punk like me, get walked
          all over all the time-- I don't stand so
          tall next to a guy like him?!

He THROWS her to the floor. Hard.

                    JODY
          Where is he, huh? Where? Ain't got no
          job. Ain't get no lovin'. Blink twice
          and you won't even have a roof over
          your head. He let you go, and told you
          he wished it kilt you. WHERE IS HE?

He grabs the framed photo of her and Indigo. SHATTERS it on the floor. Right by her.

                    JODY
          Shoot, I don't know. But I'll tell you
          where he AIN'T: Right here.

She holds the broken frame in her hand. Runs her thumb
across Indigo's face. The broken glass cuts her thumb.
Steals blood.

                    JODY
          Lookit you. Holdin' onto him ain't
          gonna bring him here to save you. All
          holdin' on to him ever did was make you
          a washed out, strung up, higher than
          twelve-noon JUNKIE.

He kneels down to her. Grabs her hard by the shoulders.
Her eyes don't leave the photo.

                    JODY
          Kicked around every day of my life,
          Chesil. Still here, ain't I? If that
          don't make me strong, too, then what am
          I?

He SHOVES her back down.

                    JODY
     WHAT AM I?

Finally, she looks at him. Hard into his soul.

                    CHESIL
          Little.

His eyes dilate with rage and embarrassment. KICKS over
the table, sending the bottle of PINOT NOIR flying.

For Chesil, everything happens in SLOW-MOTION. The
bottle, every hope she had for her and Indigo, twists and
turns in the air. As it nears the floor...

...Chesil closes her eyes. Accepting what's to come.

                                              CUT TO

INT. SPRINGS 'N' FEATHERS HOTEL- PENTHOUSE- BATHROOM-
NIGHT

Tears burst from Mack's eyes. He LAUGHS.

>   MACK THE KNIFE
>   Almost twenty women across three
>   states... over a dozen in this city
>   alone... city police, state police, even
>   the F.B.I. itself wanting a piece of
>   me... and who comes knockin'? Steve
>   McQueen looking for the WRONG GUY.

Mack LAUGHS. Harder than any man ever has. Laughs at
Indigo's quest. Laughs at the result. He falls out of the
tub, grabbing his stomach. CACKLING.

EXT. SPRINGS 'N' FEATHERS HOTEL- NIGHT

LATER. TWO COPS drag out a cuffed and naked Mack the
Knife... WHO'S STILL LAUGHING.

REPORTERS clamor around the barricade. Shooting
pictures and questions. Squid stands to the side.
Smiling. They'll never have a story better than hers.

Indigo watches as his only chance for vengeance is put in
the back of a squad car, and driven off into the horizon.

His heart pumps an awkward beat. Knocks him out of his
daze. He leans up against the side of the building. Slinks
down to the ground. As everyone clamors over the night's
events...

...Indigo sits in silence.

>   DISSOLVE TO

INT. CHESIL'S APARTMENT- LIVING ROOM- NIGHT

Indigo sits in the middle of the crime scene. At the table.

He doesn't move. Doesn't blink. He breathes, but only the minimal amount. He does nothing.

There's no more reason.

The door opens. He doesn't even twitch to see who it is: García. She looks at him. Prays she'll never understand how he feels.

> GARCÍA
> You weren't answering your cell.
> Something told me you'd be here.

She looks down. Sees his cell phone shattered on the floor.

> GARCÍA
> Oh.
>> (then)
> I know it wasn't the result you
> wanted... and I know it's embarrassing
> for both myself and the department as a
> whole, but... Thank you. For tracking
> down Mack. Helping bring him in. If
> you hadn't, who knows how many more
> he'd've... you know. Which brings me to
> why I've been calling. Why I'm here to
> see you.

Indigo doesn't care. There's nothing left for him.

> GARCÍA
> I had to fight to get Chesil's autopsy
> done in the middle of the whole Mack
> investigation. As for the results...
> yes, the beating she endured was
> severe, but it's not what killed her.

Indigo has given up. Any fight that was in him is now gone.

> GARCÍA
> In her stomach, they found traces of
> the red wine, of course. And along with

some substantial amounts of cocaine,
we found an over-the-counter
medication: Cardilexortol.

The smallest spark of life in Indigo. Barely noticeable.

                    GARCÍA
          Something for the heart, apparently. We
          tracked down her doctor. Griped about
          the whole confidentiality thing, but
          managed to tell us she did not have a
          heart condition of any sort.

Indigo goes for his breast pocket. Still wearing the same
clothes he wore when he I.D.'d the body... he pulls out the
Red Envelope. Chesil's last message.

                    GARCÍA
          With Mack the Knife in custody, we'll
          have enough legroom to further
          investigate.

If there was ever a time, it's now. Indigo opens the
Envelope. Reads the letter. His eyes go wide.

In his head, plays their song: "SIMPLE, FOOLISH WORDS" as
we...

                                        DISSOLVE TO

EXT. CHESIL'S APARTMENT BUILDING- NIGHT (FLASHBACK)

An OLD WOMAN shuts off her BLARING car alarm. She looks
up... and sees a tall man in an overcoat (Jody) running out
of the building. Turning the corner.

INT. CHESIL'S APARTMENT- LIVING ROOM- NIGHT (FLASHBACK)

Chesil lies motionless on the floor. With a cough, she
stirs to her feet. In her stumbling, she sees the envelopes
she used specifically for Indigo.

Her eyes burn holes into them. Tears and disdain. She
crumples them. Sobbing.

She goes for her purse. Pulls out a blue baggie. Searches
hard for comfort in it. When that's not enough, she pulls
out another. And another. And another.

MOMENTS LATER, and she barely exists in her own body.
Hollow and hazed through and through. In the broken
glass on the floor, her cracked reflection, she sees her
bruises and swelling. Beside that, she sees her eviction
notice.

Then, there's the bottle of PINOT NOIR. It hit the floor
when Jody kicked the table over. BUT IT DID NOT BREAK.
What was once a sign of her hope for the future, now mocks
her.

No more. No more.

Having sacrificed her body to the blue baggie, it takes
every effort to grab another envelope. To write a final
letter.

EXT. STREETS- NIGHT (FLASHBACK)

Covered in coat and hat, Chesil stumbles and limps her
way to...

INT. 24-HOUR PHARMACY- NIGHT (FLASHBACK)

She knows exactly what she wants. Finds it with ease.
Grabs it.

INT. CHESIL'S APARTMENT- LIVING ROOM- NIGHT

Though we're now in the PRESENT TIME, Indigo's
IMAGINATION continues the FLASHBACK.

IN HIS MIND'S EYE: He sees the door open. Chesil entering

with a paper bag. His eyes follow her as she takes off her hat and coat...

...and takes a seat at the table. Right across from him. He still holds the letter in his hand. Watches Chesil uncork the Pinot Noir. Pour herself a glass. And reveal what's in the bag.

CARDILEXORTOL. Indigo's heart medication. Tears flush out from his eyes as Chesil takes a handful of pills. As she does so:

She gives Indigo a look that could kill.

García is still here. Unaware of the tragic play that runs through INDIGO'S MIND. On the floor, she sees an old flyer for Chesil at Hotspot. Sighs with sympathy.

                    GARCÍA
          "Chesil Amoureux". Quite the marquee
          name. What's it mean?

Indigo gives the only answer he can.

                    INDIGO
          ...Both.

Finally we see what the letter says. The same thing Indigo told Chesil when he gave her the wine.

"I HOPE THIS KILLS YOU, TOO"

He sits there. Watching Chesil sit across the table. For the first time ever, she drinks the Pinot Noir for the exact reason they saved it for.

Something simple.

Something foolish.

                                        FADE TO BLACK

END.

—

FADE IN:

An ORB. Soft blue. Floating. Surrounded by darkness. Nothing heard but beautiful NOTES ON A PIANO. Nothing grand. Just a simple SOFT ARPEGGIO.

CUT TO

A HOUSE PARTY. Blaring HIP-HOP. HIGH SCHOOL KIDS dancing, drinking, kissing. Popping pills.

CUT TO

Surrounded by darkness, is T. He looks up at something. A SOFT BLUE LIGHT on his face: The orb. The SOFT ARPEGGIO still plays.

CUT TO

A GAME OF SPADES. A couple hundred bucks in the pot. Under the blaring HIP-HOP, kids gamble, laugh, and drink as TEENAGE DEALERS sell SMALL BAGGIES OF PILLS to their TEENAGE CUSTOMERS.

A BUYER hands some folded bills to the Dealer. Takes his baggie and casually makes for the door. The Dealer goes to count the money... "somethin' ain't right".

The Dealer says a word, and a few others in the room quickly grab the Buyer before he can leave.

CUT TO

T. Surrounded by darkness. Staring up at the floating soft-blue orb. The beautiful ARPEGGIO plays. His hands at his sides. Fingertips lightly tapping his thigh, matching the piano notes.

He's a simple dresser: white tee, blue jeans, white high-tops. Big for his age. Muscular. Soft brown eyes against a rugged visage. He's seen a lot in life.

The surrounding darkness FADES, revealing we're in--

INT. BROWNSTONE- BEDROOM- NIGHT

The "orb" is actually a LARGE BULB for a trendy lamp stand. T remains entranced by it. Unaware of the FIGHT going on behind him.

The Dealer and his boys wrestle with the Buyer. CRASHING him into the game of Spades. Struggling. The SOFT ARPEGGIO slowly MUFFLES and is replaced with the HIP-HOP, as--

T snaps out of it. Turning around to see the fight. The Dealer cuts T a look: "Do something!"

T looks down at the struggling, frightened Buyer. This isn't the first time T's had to do this. He's had to get used to the fact that it'll never be his last. He walks over to the fray... reaches for the Buyer's face, and we--

SMASH CUT TO

INT. BROWNSTONE- BATHROOM- NIGHT

Sweaty, T washes his face and the nape of his neck. On his hand, we see freshly BRUISED KNUCKLES. Water dripping down his chin, he stares into the mirror...

...and hates the monster staring back.

INT. BROWNSTONE- LIVING ROOM- NIGHT

T walks through the chaos that is teenage revelry. As he passes through: GUYS pat his back and tussle his hair, offering him a drink. GIRLS run their hands across his body, whispering in his ear, offering him drinks as well.

He declines every time. More and more they latch onto him, like bees to honey. Faster and faster he makes his way for the exit. He reaches the door, and--

EXT. BROWNSTONE- NIGHT

--walks out onto the stoop. Finally... he can breathe.

A GIRL texts on her phone while patting the back of her
vomiting BFF. A JOCK and a PLUMP NERDY GIRL surprisingly
make out.

T looks up at the sky above. Though we never see the moon,
we always see its LIGHT. Shining down on T. He takes a
moment to enjoy this. It means everything to him.

Running out of the house, is SELINA: a small duffel bag,
and short red dress. She rushes past T. Bumping into him,
taking him out of his trance. She runs across the street.

In a flash, a group of JOCKS run out after her. They catch
up to her. Grab her hard. They reach for the duffel bag,
and--

WHAM! She CLOCKS one in the face. From her form, we can
tell: she ain't new to this.

She's SHOVED to the ground. The Jocks close in on her. One
of them stops, seeing something OFF-SCREEN. He taps the
others, getting them all to look across the street at:

T. On the stoop. Watching with his tall, barrel-chested
presence.

Deciding against it, the Jocks turn and head back inside.
T remains on the stoop. Looking at Selina who's still on
the ground.

                    SELINA
        I see you've got a way with men, huh?

They just look at each other. Silent. After a beat...

                    SELINA
        You gonna help me up, or what?

T crosses the street. Helps her up.

                        SELINA
          Right in the nick of time. Don't tell me
          you got a big red "S" under that shirt.
                    (introducing)
          Selina.

He doesn't respond. Just shakes her hand.

                        SELINA
          Me, Selina. You...?

                          T
          ...T.

                        SELINA
          T? That's it?

He shrugs.

                        SELINA
          Mmkay. T. Can I get my hand back, T?

He realizes he's still shaking her hand. Lets it go.

                          T
          Sorry.

                        SELINA
          S'okay. At least you moisturize. Grabby
          McGrabHands over there, however, does
          not.

She looks at his hand. Notices the fresh bruises on his
knuckles. He realizes. Quickly pockets them.

T looks her over. The way her dark skin glows under the
moonlight. How her dress falls against her curves...

                          T
          You okay?

                        SELINA
          Sure. No worries. My clog dancing
          career is still intact.

She strikes a pose. Winces in pain. T helps her take the
weight off her ankle.

> SELINA
> Oh, no. This is it. My leg. My moves like
> Jagger. Gone forever.

She smiles at her own brand of comedy. It's completely lost
on T. After a beat...

> T
> So... I guess you wanna go to the cops,
> or someth--

> SELINA
> NO.

She quickly pulls away. Realizes her reaction. Tries to
cover.

> SELINA
> I'm fine.

He's taken aback by her response. No words to say. They
stand silent for a beat, until:

> T
> Okay. Well... see ya. I guess.

He turns. Walks back over to the brownstone.

> SELINA
> Yeah. See ya.

She watches him go. Something about him. The way he
walks, hands in his pockets. The way the moonlight hits
his body...

...she smiles.

Just as T reaches the stoop... The Buyer from before
stumbles out the door. Face BRUISED and BLOODY, thanks to
T's fists.

T and the Buyer freeze in their tracks. Stare at each other. The Buyer stands terrified. T looks at his handiwork, far from proud.

From across the street, Selina can smell the tension. So...

                    SELINA
          You wanna get outta here? House
          parties make my nipple itch.

Everyone outside, the vomiting BFF, the Plump Nerdy Girl, T-- everyone turns to her. "What??"

                    SELINA
          Just the left one, believe it or not.

She got the reaction she wanted. Walks off with a smile. Doesn't wait for an answer. As she goes:

                    SELINA
     Come on.

With options like Selina, or the house party... T chooses her. Follows behind.

                                        DISSOLVE TO

EXT. STREETS- NIGHT

T and Selina walk side by side in silence. With his hands in his pockets, T glances over at her. Trying his best to not get caught looking.

Selina catches him. More than once. She smiles to herself as they head towards a diner.

INT. GREEZY SPOON DINER- NIGHT

A full breakfast platter is placed before Selina. She twirls her fork and knife in her hands and digs in. T just sits there with a water. As Selina chows down:

                    SELINA
          You sure you're not hungry?

                      T

     Sure.

She shrugs-- "Your loss"-- and gets back to business. The
WAITER passes by, and:

                    SELINA
          Hey! I noticed a couple bottles behind
          the counter. Got any Jack?

The Waiter, a kid himself, working the late shift, gives
her a look. She's obviously underage. But the smile on her
face... "Why not?" He walks off for the counter.

                    SELINA
          You're a doll!
                (then; to T)
          So. What school you go to?

T prepares himself. It's not a question he likes
answering. Regardless:

                      T

     Gamarra.

She stops. Fork only inches from her mouth. She looks at
him as if he worked at the Twin Towers.

                    SELINA
          Gamarra High? "Gomorrah"??

He bites his tongue to the "nickname".

                    SELINA
          How do you like it there?

                      T
     It's high school. Nothing much to it.

                    SELINA
          Yeah, but... I mean, it's got a rep.

T shrugs. Staring at his water.

                    T
          It's high school.

Selina takes the hint. Moves on.

                    SELINA
          Party often?

                    T
          Not really. Didn't plan on being there,
          but...

                    SELINA
          Just happened, huh?

                    T
          Something like that. You?

                    SELINA
          Nah. Just a pit stop, actually.

                    T
          Where you headed?

                    SELINA
          Bus terminal. Connecticut.

                    T
          This late? How come your mom didn't
          drop you off?

                    SELINA
          Cuz I'm a big girl, and I can handle
          myself. And why do kids always say
          "mom" instead of "dad", or "parents"?
          It's like they EXPECT you not to have a
          father in the picture.

                    T
          Okay. How come your parents didn't
          drop you off?

                              SELINA
              I told you. I'm a big girl. My parents
              raised me differently. "Alternative
              parenting" kinda thing. They're not on
              my back about everything, looking
              over my shoulder. They treat me like an
              adult, let me make my own choices.

                                 T
              And as an "adult", you decided to go to
              Connecticut this late at night?

                              SELINA
              When ELSE am I gonna see the moon? You
              ever been?

                                 T
              To the moon?

                              SELINA
              No, stupid. Connecticut.

                                 T
              Oh. Yeah. My grandmother lived out
              there.

                              SELINA
              Lived?

                                 T
              ...Yeah.

He sips his water. Selina understands.

                              SELINA
              Oh.

T shrugs it off. Accustomed to burying it. The Waiter
returns with a glass of Jack. A heavy pour. Selina thanks
him, slapping his butt as he walks off.

T stares into his water. His mind somewhere else. By now,
we notice a SONG playing over the radio. T's finger taps
the glass in unison. Head nodding ever so slightly.

Selina clocks all of this.

                    SELINA
              (re: whiskey)
          You could've ordered one, you know. He
          seems cool.

                    T
          Nah.

                    SELINA
          Want a sip?

                    T
          I'm good. Thanks.

She raises an eyebrow.

                    T
          I don't drink.

                    SELINA
          Laaaaame. Wait, is it, like a... religion
          thing, or something?

                    T
          ...Yeah.

                    SELINA
          Oh. That's cool. Don't get me wrong, it's
          still lame, but, whatever. Do you.

T chuckles a bit as he sips his water. Trying to hide it.

                    SELINA
          Oh! He laughs!

The SONG slips him back into silence. Lulling him.
Instinctively, his lips silently move along with it:

"I feel the light that shines in
Sparkling high over sea
When the time comes, when the time comes
I know I'll be free..."

Selina softly smiles at the sight of T in his own world.
Fingertips tapping a distinctive rhythm on the table.

The Waiter returns with the bill. T goes for his wallet,
but Selina reaches out. Stopping him.

                    SELINA
          Nah-uh, sweetheart...

She pulls out a FAT WAD OF CASH.

                    SELINA
          ...I gots this.

EXT. STREETS- NIGHT

They walk on their way. T's hands back in his pockets. He
takes a chance. Closes the gap between him and Selina. She
notices. Doesn't say anything.

                    T
          So. Your mom hooked you up with all
          that cash?

                    SELINA
          My parents wanted to... but I decided to
          make my way out of town all on my own.
          So, if you MUST know, I am a
          Resourceful Financial Opportunist.

Beat. T looks at her.

                    T
          You're a thief?

                    SELINA
          Tuh! Such a nasty word...

T sucks his teeth. Playfully dismissing her. She punches
him in the shoulder. He laughs it off.

                    SELINA
          I am! Honest! Why do you think those
          guys were after me?

                    T
          Please. A girl like you? Come on...

                    SELINA
          "A girl like"--??

She punches him in the shoulder. Harder.

                    T
          You better not.

                    SELINA
          Or what?

She hits him again. Puts her dukes up. Bounces up and
down like an old Irish boxer.

                    SELINA
          You saw me clock that guy in the face.

                    T
          Also saw his boy throw you down.

                    SELINA
          You're twice his size. This should be
          easy, then.

She hits him. Again. And again. Throws another hit, that
he blocks. Throws another one. He blocks that, too.

                    SELINA
          Ooooh... Not too shabby.

They go back and forth. Taking playful swings at each
other. Tapping each other's chins. T manages to grab hold
of both Selina's wrists. Presses her firmly against a
parked car.

                    T
          Call it.

                         112

                    SELINA
        I win.

                       T
        What? How?

Selina softly raises her knee to T's crotch. A playful
threat. He gets the message.

                       T
        You win.

He lets her go. They take a moment to catch their breaths.

                       T
        You know how to fight.

                    SELINA
        Beautiful girl like me in a town like
        this? Of course. But, you...

T shrugs.

                    SELINA
        Clearly something you picked up at
        Gomorrah. You fight a lot?

He doesn't answer.

                    SELINA
        That why those guys were scared of
        you?

They stand in silence. T can't answer that. He just walks
on. Selina follows after him. Intrigued.

They head down a shadowed block. Selina playfully trying
to not get caught looking over at T. He catches her. She
gives up. Laughing.

                    SELINA
        The girls at school have this much fun
        with you?

T turns away. Bashful.

                    SELINA
          Ahh! So they DO. Lemme guess: is she an
          Ashley? Or a Kaija? Probably a
          Meredith.

T cuts her a look. "What??" She laughs.

                    SELINA
          Nope! I know! She's probably a Jasmine
          with a Z, or even worse: Unique, but
          with a K.

T laughs. Not much, but the most he's done so far.

                    SELINA
          Yes! So it IS Unique with a K!

                    T
          Na-uh. Don't put that on me.

                    SELINA
          Oh, my God, five minutes I've known
          you, I'm already disappointed in your
          taste. I had such high standards for
          you.

                    T
          I'm pretty sure no one has a name like
          that.

                    SELINA
          I'm pretty sure if there was, she'd
          DEFINITELY go to Gomorrah.

                    T
          Don't... don't call it that.

                    SELINA
          You guys call it that.

                    T
          No, we don't. Just...

                    SELINA
        Sorry. I've just always heard things
        about it. Never actually met someone
        who goes there. Everyone's got a
        brother or a cousin who does-- or at
        least USED TO until he got arrested,
        or, you know... shot.

                       T
        Ta-da. I guess.

                    SELINA
        My bad. You like it there, so I
        shouldn't--

                       T
        I didn't say I liked it. Just said it's
        high school. Like any other.

                    SELINA
        Mmkay, there's inaccurate... and then
        there's what you just said.

T cuts her a look.

                    SELINA
        I'm just saying... there's only ONE
        PLACE in history that God got so mad
        at, He did what Left Eye did to Andre
        Rison... and there's only ONE PLACE
        named after it.

T can't help but to laugh a little.

                       T
        Alright. You got it.

                    SELINA
        Ha! Thank you, kindly.

They round the corner. Back under the soothing rays of
the OFF-SCREEN moon. Just knowing it's up there, T
glances up at it. Something takes over him, and--

                              T
                You should see it at night, though...

                          SELINA
                You've been to your school at night?

                              T
                Couple times.

She stops in her tracks.

                              T
                What?

Smiles from ear to ear.

                              T
                What?

Her smile remains. It finally dawns on him.

                              T
                No.

                          SELINA
                Oh, come on...

                              T
                Nooo...

                          SELINA
                Please....?

She pouts. T is immune, at first... Eventually, he sighs,
and we--

                                          DISSOLVE TO

INT. GAMARRA HIGH- HALLWAY- NIGHT

Moonlight seeps through the windows. The halls partially
illuminate with an eerie, yet magical feel. Foreboding,
yet welcoming.

A loose window pane is removed. T and Selina, no more
than two shadows in the night, quietly enter. T is first,
sticking the landing perfectly. Selina stumbles through,
giggling.

                         T
          Shh!

                      SELINA
          You shh.

Selina looks down the hall. Sees the delicate mixture of
light and dark. The way the windows reflect the
moonlight. How every turning corner seeps into
mysterious shadow. She stands taken aback by it all.

                         T
          Grand tour.

As they walk through, Selina runs her fingers along the
wall. Notices a DEEP SCRATCH.

                         T
          Lawrence found out Josh was with his
          girl during Senior Trip. Snuck a blade
          in to clear up the misunderstanding.

She notices a CRACKED WINDOW.

                         T
          Rashaad pulled a prank on Caitlin.
          Rubbed Nair on her head. She took HIS
          head, and--

                      SELINA
          Oh, God, please, no mor--

T grabs her by the arm. Stoping her.

                         T
          Don't step there.

                      SELINA
          ...Do I wanna know why?

They carefully walk over the spot. Keep on down the hall.

                    SELINA
          What was that song?

                    T
          What song?

                    SELINA
          Back at the diner. An oldie, or
          something. You knew it. Just didn't
          figure you for the type.

                    T
          Victim of circumstance, I guess. My
          grandma. She played stuff like that all
          the time.

                    SELINA
          Aw... spent nights with her by the fire?
          Listening to her old 45?

                    T
          Hated it back then, actually. Nina
          Simone, Al Green, Otis Redding...

                    SELINA
          Oh, trust me, I know. They all sound the
          same. And they're so slow. Like, crazy
          slow. Sad, too.

                    T
          Nah. I mean... yeah, but... more than
          that. Y'know?

                    SELINA
          I would LOVE to, but you're gonna have
          to give me more than caveman grunts.

                    T
          Those songs... you listen to them once,
          and, yeah, they're slow. But listen to
          them again, and you realize they were
          just taking advantage of every moment.

Savoring it. And at first, they sound
sad and all, but sooner or later, you
understand they're just full of heart.
Hopeful sometimes. Y'know? Like they
feel everything so we don't have to.

She smiles at his analysis. Did not see that coming. T
blushes, and, as if apologizing:

                    T
They remind me of her, I guess. Didn't
really know it then, but that dusty
45... the way the moon sat behind the
pine trees, shining through, putting
me to sleep every night... best times of
my life before I moved back here.

Beat.

                 SELINA
One hundred and three.

                    T
What?

                 SELINA
You just said one hundred and three
words straight through.

                    T
There's no way you counted all that.

                 SELINA
First of all, prove it. Then of all,
don't bother, cuz I still watch Sesame
Street, so I'm basically Good Will
Hunting. Also of all... I think I'm
growing on you, T.

He tries to hide his blush.

                 SELINA
Wait. "Before you moved BACK here?" So
you were here, then moved to

Connecticut, then moved back? Why'd
you have to move there in the first
place?

He shrugs.

                    T
          Stuff.

                    SELINA
          Like stuff-stuff, or the garden variety
          kinda stuff?

                    T
          Stuff.

Heavy. She presses no further. They walk on.

                                        DISSOLVE TO

INT. GAMARRA HIGH- AUDITORIUM- NIGHT

They enter. She opens her arms and twirls. Taking in the
grandness of the Coliseum-like room: massive stage,
numerous seats, and a GRAND PIANO.

                    SELINA
          This is amazing! My school's nowhere
          near as big as this.

She takes T by the hands. Twirls him down and down the
aisle. Faster and faster, yelping and laughing. They reach
the stage and try their best to stay on their feet. Dizzy.

She sees the massive stage before her. A kid in a candy
shop, she quickly runs up. Clicks her heels. Puts her
finger under her nose: Hitler's mustache.

                    SELINA
          Achtung! Ze students vill take zeir
          seats, and vill not disturb ze
          performance! Qvickly!

                       120

T takes a seat in the front row. Pretending he's not interested. Selina runs backstage. After a beat... she walks back on. A different character. Powerful. She turns to T, and:

> SELINA
> Cannon to the right of them!
> Cannon to the left of them!
> Cannon in front of them
> Volley'd and thunder'd;
> Storm'd at with shot and shell
> Boldly they rode and well,
> Into the jaws of Death,
> Into the mouth of Hell
> Rode the six hundred!

Then, slowly, tantalizingly, singing like Marilyn Monroe:

> SELINA
> Conjunction Junction
> What's your function...

She thrusts her hands into her stomach. With a groan she falls to her knees. Panting. Gasping.

> SELINA
> Eh tu... Brutus...?

She looks over at T. Frowns her lips like Al Pacino. Mimics his every hand gesture.

> SELINA
> Just when I thought I was out... they
> pull me back IN...

She falls. "Dead". Then rolls onto her side, her back facing T. Coyly looking over her shoulder:

> SELINA
> Draw me like one of your French girls,
> Jack.

And scene. T gives her a standing ovation. Whistles. Selina runs over to the podium. She looks around, gaping

as if there's a whole audience clapping for her. Just like
Sally Field at the Oscars:

>   SELINA
>   You like me! You really like me!

T goes over to the stage and offers his hand, helping her
down. She sits on the piano. T takes a seat in front of it.
Glancing at the keys as he does so.

>   T
>   You're crazy, you know that?

>   SELINA
>   What a coincidence-- my therapist
>   says the same thing.

>   T
>   You should listen to him.

>   SELINA
>   Her. And, honestly, if she was so smart,
>   she'd have gotten a Bachelorette's
>   instead of a Bachelor's. Boop.

T laughs. A bit louder than before. It's a good one. Hearty.
Genuine. The kind you long to hear again. Selina smiles.

>   SELINA
>   The acoustics in this room... God...

>   T
>   Amazing, huh?

>   SELINA
>   I see why you come here.

Outside, a cloud shifts. Moonlight pours in. Painting T's
skin with quality oil.

>   SELINA
>   Play something.

                    T
          Oh, I... I don't--

                 SELINA
          Yeah, you do.

                    T
          No, really, I--

                 SELINA
          Come on. You looked for Middle C before
          you sat down. You play. Lemme hear.

T's caught. He positions his fingers. Plays stiltedly: MA.
RY. HAD. A. LIT. TLE. LAMB.

Selina just looks at him. Knows there's more he's hiding.
She doesn't have to say a word. T gives in... and the same
hands with bruised knuckles plays the SOFT ARPEGGIO we
heard in the beginning. The beautiful notes wrap around.
Repeating again and again.

T sings. His voice is untrained. Yet, flows like warm
velvet.

                    T
          Light through the pines
          'member how you used to glow?
          Light through the pines
          How things were so long ago?

          Your shine
          It used to be a smile for only you and
          me
          But now, what was
          Can never be

He finishes. Selina looks at him with a smile.

                 SELINA
          Play it again, Sam.

No one's ever told him that before. With more confidence,
he plays and sings it from the top. But, when he reaches

the end...

                         T
          Your shine
          It used to me a smile for only you and
          me

...Selina cuts in with her own:

                       SELINA
          But now, it seems
          Like you smile for three...

Those two lines change the song entirely. Taking the turn
from mournful, to hopeful. He continues the notes. Selina,
off the top of her head:

                       SELINA
          Light through the pines
          Been a while since we last spoke
          Up late at night
          And something something something
          else that rhymes with "spoke"

They laugh.

                       SELINA
          Wish I was free
          As free as you are
          Hanging high up in the night

          To fly

                         T
          To give

                       SELINA
          To sing

                         T
          To live

                         SELINA
             To hide from the world, from the cold
             Break out of the mold
             To smile with my heart and live
             forever

                            T
             To start fresh, return to the past
             And spend it with you

Impressed with their simpatico spontaneity, they sing it
again. Realizing the meaning as they go along. Together.

                        T/ SELINA
             To hide from the world, from the cold
             Break out of the mold
             To smile with my heart and live
             forever
             To start fresh, return to the past...

                            T
             To shine through the pines

He plays the last note. They sit there. Looking into each
other's eyes. As the last note whispers out into the
moonlight, we...

                                        DISSOLVE TO

INT. GAMARRA HIGH- 3RD FLOOR- NIGHT

T stands. Facing a wall. Can't believe he's doing this.

                            T
             Un. Real.

Very faintly, we HEAR:

                       SELINA (O.S.)
             Come on!

T sighs, and...

                         T
Marco.

                    SELINA (O.S.)
You have to say it louder.

                         T
You OBVIOUSLY heard me.

                    SELINA (O.S.)
Louder!

                         T
Marco!

                    SELINA (O.S.)
Polo!

He walks off in search for Selina. Calling "Marco" as she
screams "Polo".

He turns for down the hallway... but opts for the staircase
instead. He walks up. Slowly.

INT. GAMARRA HIGH- CLASSROOM- NIGHT

Selina sits under the teacher's desk. Giggling to herself.
Trying to stay quiet. In the distance, we hear T calling
"Marco".

Quickly, she gets up and runs to the door. Sees T's head
pass through the staircase.

INT. GAMARRA HIGH- 4TH FLOOR- NIGHT

Selina runs, heading for a SECOND STAIRCASE. She rounds
the corner just as T exits. He spots her.

                         T
Hey, you said "no running", Marco!

INT. GAMARRA HIGH- STAIRCASE- NIGHT

Selina slides down the banister. Laughing all the way
down.

                    SELINA
          Polooooo...!!

INT. GAMARRA HIGH- 4TH FLOOR- NIGHT

T runs past the staircase Selina went through. Thinking
she's still on the same floor as him. Laughing as:

"Marco!"

"Polo!"

"Marco!"

                    SELINA (O.S.)
          AAAHHH!!!

T screeches to a stop. Whipping around as Selina's scream
ECHOES throughout the building.

                    T
          ...Selina?

INT. GAMARRA HIGH- 3RD FLOOR- NIGHT

Selina presses herself up against the wall. Panting.

A DARK SHADOW quickly soars past her, and--

INT. GAMARRA HIGH- 4TH FLOOR- NIGHT

T's face crumbles as he hears Selina's BLOOD-CURDLING
SCREAM.

                                T
        SELINA!

He takes off. Running for:

INT. GAMARRA HIGH- STAIRCASE- NIGHT

He heads down a couple of stairs, but stops. Hears her
SCREAM again. He knows it's coming from downstairs. Bolts
UPstairs instead.

                                T
        Hang on!

INT. GAMARRA HIGH- 3RD FLOOR- NIGHT

Selina runs as fast as she can. Honest terror splashed on
her face.

INT. GAMARRA HIGH- 5TH FLOOR- NIGHT

T bursts out of the staircase. Runs for the far end of the
hall. Practically flying. Goes over to a locker. Tries to
work the lock, but his hands keep slipping off the knob.

BAM! BAM! BAM! Punches the locker. No use. Grabs hold of
the lock and pulls... Pulls... PULLS, until finally, it pops
open.

Inside, are BAGGIES OF PILLS, ENVELOPES OF CASH... and a
GLOCK 9.

INT. GAMARRA HIGH- STAIRCASE- NIGHT

T bursts through the doors. Jumping clean over the stairs.
Slamming into the wall. He presses forward. Gun in hand.

                              128

INT. GAMARRA HIGH- 3RD FLOOR- NIGHT

He carefully exits the staircase. Gun leveled right in
front of him. The way he holds it... it's not his first time.
He fights his heavy breathing.

                    T
          Selina?

The floor is dark. No windows for moonlight to come
through. An open door down the hall reveals a STREAK OF
LIGHT on the floor. He moves quietly across. Ghostlike. We
see the room is marked: SWIM TEAM.

INT. GAMARRA HIGH- SWIM ROOM- NIGHT

A MASSIVE SWIMMING POOL sits in the center. The moon's
rays flush in from the elongated row of tall windows.
Hitting the swaying pool water, creating a hypnotic
"disco ball" effect on the walls.

T enters carefully. Sees Selina sitting at the edge of the
pool. Head down, buried in her hands. He takes one step
towards her, and--

FWOOSH! The dark shadow flutters past. T trains his gun on
it. Sees it's a couple of PIGEONS. Trapped inside.

He lowers the gun. Laughs a bit. Looks back at Selina...
and the look of embarrassment on her face dies his
laughter down.

He keeps the smile as he walks over to her. Sits down next
to her.

                    T
          It's dark. I'd've screamed, too.

She turns her head away from him. Far too embarrassed to
even look at him. He rests the gun on the floor. Walks over
to the windows.

Selina looks at the gun. A different kind of fear now

washing over her.

T opens the window. Moonlight flushes in like never before. The pigeons fly out into the sky. Free. We PULL BACK TO:

T and Selina. So small in this large room. The moonlight reflecting off the swaying water, like large, blueish fireflies. Dancing around the two.

And the gun.

DISSOLVE TO

INT. GAMARRA HIGH- CLASSROOM- NIGHT

CLOSE ON a desk drawer. Locked. Selina's hand comes in with a screwdriver. Uses it as leverage. Breaks in. From inside the drawer, Selina's hand pulls out...

...a small bottle of VODKA.

INT. GAMARRA HIGH- SWIM ROOM- NIGHT

Selina enters, bottle in hand. Walks to the far side of the pool, next to T.

                    SELINA
          You were right. Your Math teacher DOES
          have a drinking problem.

                    T
          I know an alckie when I see one.

Selina takes a seat next to him as she sips. She offers, but he declines.

T holds out his phone to her.

                    SELINA
          Oh. Is this how you asked Unique with a
          K?

He sucks his teeth. Starts to put his phone back in his
pocket. Selina takes it from him. Dials in her number. He
pockets it. Stares down at the pool.

                    SELINA
          Ever try to join the team?

                      T
          Don't have one. Not anymore, at least.
          Used to go statewide. Win first place,
          and stuff.
                    (shrugs)
          Before I came.

                    SELINA
          What happened?

As T answers, he takes off his shoes and socks. Gently puts
his feet in the water. Her eyes memorize every detail.

                      T
          Life. Things started getting crazy.
          Kids getting mixed up with this crew,
          that crew, whatever. All the issues
          with that, money for the team stopped.
          You ask me, money for the whole school
          stopped, too. Rent the pool out for
          community swim lessons on the weekend
          just to keep the lights on.

Selina looks out through the window. The moon isn't
visible, but its rays are. Glistening against the rippling
pool, thanks to T's swaying, immersed feet. She smiles at
the beauty of the night sky, as...

T lays down on his back. Feet still in the water. He looks
up at Selina. Her full, natural hair. The moonlight
causing the tip of her nose and the curves of her face to
glow. He reaches out. Softly touches her arm with his
fingertips.

                     131

Up and down her arm, his fingertips slide. Selina closes
her eyes. Feeling his touch ripple through her every
nerve.

A question dawns on her. He can feel it.

                         T
            What's up?

                       SELINA
            The gun... Where'd it come from?

The gun still sits on the floor. The far other side of the
pool. Away from them. As if that makes it better.

                         T
            It's high school. Always a gun
            somewhere.

                       SELINA
            No. No, there isn't. And even IF... how'd
            you know exactly where it was?

Caught, T removes his hand from Selina's arm. Looks back
at the night sky.

                       SELINA
            So, everything I heard about this
            place... you're like, what? Involved?

T just lies there. The moon reflecting off his eyes.

                       SELINA
            Is that why those guys were so scared
            of you?

She doesn't let up, does she? T sighs. Lifts his shirt.
Shows a TATTOO on his chest. A FLAMING SKULL.

                         T
            Los Muertos Vivos. Snatched me up
            pretty quick. Always was kinda big for
            my age.

He tries to shrug it off. Clocks the look of disapproval
and discomfort on her face.

                    T
               (scoffs)
     Wow.

                    SELINA
          Sorry, it's just... I mean, the stuff they
          do...

                    T
          I'm not down with that. And this is
          coming from a girl who's, what,
          sixteen, chugging a vodka?

                    SELINA
          "Chugging"? Why is it-- first of all,
          I'm seventeen.

                    T
          Oh, my bad. You look so young for a
          full-grown adult.

                    SELINA
          Whatever. And why is it every time a
          person who doesn't drink sees someone
          else take a sip, they act like the other
          guy's an alcoholic, or something?

                    T
          If you're not already, it's where you're
          headed.

                    SELINA
          Ha! Imagine what YOU'RE headed for.

                    T
          I TOLD YOU, I'm not down with stuff like
          that. I don't sling, I don't go around
          killing people--

                    SELINA
          You've got their tat on your chest--
          you go around doing SOMETHING.

She takes his hand. Shows him his bruised knuckles. Then,
softly...

                    SELINA
          You're better than that, T.

He sits up. Offended.

                    T
          What do YOU know about ME?

                    SELINA
          As much as YOU know about ME to call me
          an alcoholic. And that's STILL more
          than enough for me to say that you're
          better-- that ANYONE'S better than a
          group of kids going around calling
          themselves THE LIVING DEAD.

                    T
          You don't know enough of anything.

                    SELINA
          Then, tell me.

                    T
          Why? So you could gimme that look,
          again? Same way everybody ELSE looks
          at me when they find out I go to school
          here? Cuz I just GOTTA be "one of THEM",
          right?

                    SELINA
               (under breath)
          Clearly you are.

                    T
          HEY. I don't have the freedom of being
          better than cash in my pocket. I don't
          have the freedom of protection on the

                         134

street, or "alternative parenting", and I DEFINITELY don't have the freedom to pack up and leave my family behind. In my family, I'M the parent.

Beat. That's the most he's ever raised his voice. Taking her by surprise. They just sit there. Looking at each other. Emotions high.

T turns away. Too much has been shared. Needs that wall back up. Selina realizes. Breaks the awkward silence first.

> SELINA
> My mom's a forty-three year old little girl. She thinks every man she meets is gonna be "the one". The one strong enough to finally save her from herself. Save her from my dad... who wouldn't be able to bother her if she'd just TELL the cops what he does. If she'd stop listening to him every time he says he's "sorry". Just about as "alternative" as their parenting gets.

T doesn't react to this "revelation". Almost as if he's always known.

> T
> Why Connecticut?

> SELINA
> Honestly? Boston, L.A., Wisconsin, even. I don't care. As long as it's away from here. As long as it's a piece of what was. How things used to be before...
> (sighs)
> ...everything else.

> T
> "Light through the pines".

Tears swell. She smiles widely. They know so little of each other... yet more than anyone else, T understands.

                    SELINA
Come with me.

                    T
What?

                    SELINA
Connecticut. Or Boston, or L.A., or
wherever-- come with me.

                    T
I can't.

                    SELINA
Why not? Los Muertos--?

                    T
No, not them.

                    SELINA
Then, why not?

He touches her cheek. Caressing her skin with his thumb.

                    T
I don't have the freedom.

That breaks her. She does a great job of holding together
despite it. Then, as if this was always the conversation to
begin with...

                    T
Theodore.

She laughs at the name...

                    SELINA
Teddy.

...and leans in for a kiss. Just before their lips touch--

--T pushes Selina into the pool. She shrieks, laughing as
he jumps in after her. They splash water in each other's
faces. Giggling like they're in kindergarten.

                          136

Underwater. The two stand on the pool floor. His hands on her hips. Her arms around his neck. Dancing in the deep end. Her red dress flows like a vision. In this moment...

...they find peace.

DISSOLVE TO

INT. TRAIN- NIGHT

A HOMELESS MAN tries to sleep. Can't, thanks to T and Selina running up and down. Swirling and twirling on the safety poles. Laughing with each other.

INT. BUS TERMINAL- NIGHT

Holding her duffel bag for her, T and Selina walk through the station. Still laughing. Getting as much of each other until they can no longer.

They reach the bus, already loading. He hands her the bag. She slings it over her shoulder, her eyes never leaving his. She's been waiting for this. Rests her hand on his chest, above his heart. Tip-toes up and kisses him.

A sweet, passionate, everlasting kiss goodbye.

She walks onto the line. Fingertips lingering on his chest as she turns away. Standing on the line, she tosses him a small black object. He catches it.

A WALLET.

FLASHBACK: Greezy Spoon Diner. Selina slaps the waiter on the butt.

She really IS a thief.

T walks off with a smile. Leaving Selina on the line.

On the escalator, heading up to the exit, T is lost in

thought. As he rises... he softly touches his lips. Right where Selina kissed him.

The moonlight casts down on him. He looks up at it. It's the same moonlight as before... yet different. A sign, almost.

He runs back down.

Selina moves up on the line.

T cuts through a large platform. Flying, almost. Making his way through.

Selina reaches the bus door. Ticket in hand.

T runs. Faster than ever before. A smile growing on his face.

Selina turns to look at US. A smile of hope on her face.

CUT TO

T reaches. The platform is empty. The bus heads off into the distance. For a second, T is broken. He recovers: pulls out his cell phone.

It's dead. Streaks of water on it from his dive in the pool.

He stands there. Watching as the bus disappears.

DISSOLVE TO

Time has passed. T is still here. Waiting. Not sure for what. Just waiting. Hoping.

Eventually, he moves on.

EXT. STREETS- NIGHT

He walks on his way. And without Selina, everything seems a bit emptier.

INT. T'S APARTMENT- LIVING ROOM- NIGHT

He enters. It's small. Cluttered. Restrictive. As he walks
through, his foot hits a bottle. Further in, there are
other empty bottles and cans of alcohol. On the couch...

...his FATHER. Passed out. A bottle barely hanging from his
fingertips. He takes the sheet bundled at his father's
feet. Covers him with it.

There's a reason why he doesn't drink. It's not religious.

INT. T'S APARTMENT- BEDROOM- NIGHT

Dark. T enters especially quiet. A sleeping six-year old
in the bed. His BROTHER.

T crawls in beside him. He lays there. Staring into the
darkness. The clouds outside part...

...and moonlight pours in. Revealing an old YAMAHA
KEYBOARD in the corner. Taking his headphones from the
bedside dresser, T plugs it into the keyboard.

Looks for Middle C as he sits.

With his headphones in his ears, sitting in the shower of
moonlight... T plays. The same SOFT ARPEGGIO we heard
before. A smile on his face. Happier than when we first met
him.

Something in him has changed.

                                        DISSOLVE TO

In all its shining, glorious splendor, finally we see...

THE MOON.

                                        FADE TO BLACK

END.

FROM THE BLACK:

                        SANDS MARQUEE (V.O.)
            Define "love". Go ahead. Define it. If
            someone's face, name, or even the touch
            of their lips pops into your mind...
            you're screwed.

Slender, manicured FINGERS run through a full head of
HAIR. Primping.

                        SANDS MARQUEE (V.O.)
            For the sole reason that every single
            person on the face of this earth will
            one day die, you are screwed.

Raspberry red LIPSTICK coats a lush pair of LIPS.

                        SANDS MARQUEE (V.O.)
            They will die, and all you'll be left
            with is their face, their name, and the
            overly-romanticized memory of their
            lips. Lips you will never touch again.

NEEDLE AND THREAD snake through BLACK CLOTH. Hemming.

                        SANDS MARQUEE (V.O.)
            You will grieve. You will cry. You will
            mourn.

A SNUB-NOSE REVOLVER. The slender, manicured fingers
snap open the cylinder. Empty.

                        SANDS MARQUEE (V.O.)
            And then, you'll remarry. Re-engage.
            Re-love.

A BULLET is plugged in. Another...

                        SANDS MARQUEE (V.O.)
            Then, the next time you hear the word
            "love", you will think of someone else.
            Someone else's face. Someone else's
            name. Someone else's lips.

...and another. SIX total.

                    SANDS MARQUEE (V.O.)
          And the second person you abandoned
          the memory of your first love for...
          will eventually abandon the memory of
          you, and love someone else.

Fully loaded, the cylinder is snapped shut. Placed in a
CLUTCH.

                    SANDS MARQUEE (V.O.)
          You expect me to say something
          profoundly beautiful about love.
          Truth is...

HEELS are slipped on. Black. Red bottom. She who wears
them is now taller. Harder. Deadlier.

                    SANDS MARQUEE (V.O.)
          ...I honestly don't know the first
          profoundly beautiful thing about it.

THE WOMAN walks out the door with the clutch. She closes
it behind her, as we...

                                        FADE OUT

                    SANDS MARQUEE (V.O.)
          No one does.

EXT. STREETS- NIGHT

She walks on her way. An expert in the art of high heels.
Without even hailing for one, a TAXI CAB pulls up,
partially mounting the curb.

She gets in.

INT. TAXI CAB- NIGHT

Stifling darkness. The brief lights of passing street

lamps graces the CABBIE with glimpses of Her. A wild and
raucous body. Contained and controlled in her dress and
self-respect.

She looks out the window. Eyeing the city that rolls past:
Shady deals. Muggings. Alleyway activity. Bodies under
white tarps. Behind crime scene tapes.

Too many.

EXT. SPRINGS 'N' FEATHERS HOTEL- NIGHT

The cab pulls up. She gets out.

The building is dimly lit. Old and decrepit. No one with
any dignity would dare enter. And if they did, they'd pay
by the hour.

INT. SPRINGS 'N' FEATHERS HOTEL- LOBBY- NIGHT

Standing by the entrance, She examines the room:

In one corner, an OLDER MAN in a three-piece suit. TWO
WOMEN rub his shoulders, loosen his tie.

Another corner, a YOUNG MAN sits nervous and excited.
ANOTHER WOMAN whispers in his ear. Slowly takes off his
WEDDING RING.

There are others. Most with specific requirements for the
night. Some who take whatever they can afford.

Our Woman nods. This will do quite nicely.

She walks over to the FRONT DESK CLERK, talking and
giggling with him. Her demeanor has changed: now bubbly,
immature, and hormonal.

The Front Desk Clerk looks at a list in a notebook. Room
numbers with checkmarks next to them. All except for room
704.

The Woman heads off. Trailing the fingers of her left hand on the counter, tantalizing the Front Desk Clerk... while her right hand dials a number on her CELL PHONE.

She dumps the cell in the garbage bin, and enters the elevator.

INT. SPRINGS 'N' FEATHERS HOTEL- ROOM 704- NIGHT

"704": a sweet-faced, white bearded fella. He opens the door for The Woman, who's already dropped her bubbly persona. She's back to how we first met her: Hard.

She sits on the bed, and "704" takes a seat beside her. While he looks at Her longingly, she looks through her clutch. Disinterested. Maybe even disgusted. He touches the zipper on her dress, and--

--she sprays him with MACE from her clutch. He falls to the floor, writhing in pain. From her clutch, she takes out a pair of HANDCUFFS. Locks his wrist and ankle around the bed leg.

She pulls the revolver from her clutch. Rips off a corner of the bed sheet, ties the gun high up on her inner thigh.

Our Woman goes over to the mini-bar. Grabs three small VODKAS. She walks back to the bed. Lies down with a sigh. Kicks off her heels.

Eyes closed, she guzzles the vodkas. All three at once. She doesn't stop until the bottles are empty. When they are, she doesn't cough. Doesn't so much as clear her throat.

DISSOLVE TO

INSIDE THE LOBBY GARBAGE CAN: Her cell phone. The line has been open for eight minutes... to 911.

INT. SPRINGS 'N' FEATHERS HOTEL- LOBBY- NIGHT

Two cops, VETERAN and ROOKIE, enter. They take one look
at the lobby, and know what kinda joint this is.

They round everyone up. Backup is called. Veteran Cop
grills the Front Desk Clerk. He breaks, and reveals the
list of "special" hotel rooms.

INT. SPRINGS 'N' FEATHERS HOTEL- VARIOUS ROOMS- NIGHT

Doors are kicked open. Occupants exposed. Midnight
conversations interrupted.

INT. SPRINGS 'N' FEATHERS HOTEL- ROOM 704- NIGHT

The same for this room. UNIFORMED COPS enter to see "704"
still on the floor, cuffed. The Woman is still on the bed.
Waiting. Drinking. The cops move in to cuff her.

Her name is SANDS MARQUEE. And her night is just getting
started, as we...

FADE OUT

18 HOURS EARLIER...

A CELL PHONE on a bedside dresser. Beside it, we see the
muscled back of a MAN in bed. The alarm goes off, waking
him. He rolls over, and shuts off the phone. PULL BACK TO
REVEAL we're in:

INT. COPPER'S APARTMENT- BEDROOM- DAY

Simple. The bare necessities: bed, half-mirror, small TV
set, and curtains.

COPPER COLT lies on his back, on the far side of the bed.
The other side untouched. Bare. He reaches over and
touches the empty space. Trying to feel the warmth of

someone no longer there.

The VOID pains him terribly. Even more so as a SLIVER OF
SUNLIGHT cuts through between the curtains. The sliver
falls across his left hand, his bare RING FINGER.
Mirroring what was once there.

INT. COPPER'S APARTMENT- BATHROOM- DAY

He showers. A slow, tired routine. His life is deafeningly
silent, except for the water clapping against his body.

His body is hard and coarse. Big hands. Bigger chest. But,
his eyes: Wounded. Hurting.

INT. COPPER'S APARTMENT- BEDROOM- DAY

He dresses. Shirt and tie. A NEWS REPORT on the T.V.

                    NEWS REPORT
          --investigation into Detective
          Sergeant Sticky Palmer is still
          ongoing, with sources in the District
          Attorney's Office revealing that his
          alibi was not-- I repeat-- WAS NOT
          corroborated by his own partner,
          Detective Copper Co--

Copper turns it off. As he walks off, we see the waist of his
slacks.

.45 PISTOL. GOLD BADGE.

EXT. STREETS- DAY

Copper walks on his way, coffee in hand. Bleak despite the
sunshine. GASPS and SCREAMS are heard OFF-SCREEN. He
hurries over to see:

A FATHER on the ground, holding his bleeding head in

pain. Shards of a BROKEN BOTTLE around him. A MOTHER
kneels beside him. Copper runs over, showing his badge.

                    COPPER COLT
          What happened?

                    MOTHER
          My son, he... it was just an argument
          and he... He's not well. He has a
          condition, he doesn't handle--

                    COPPER COLT
          Which way, ma'am?

                    MOTHER
          You can't hurt him, he's--

                    COPPER COLT
          Ma'am, which way?

                    MOTHER
                 (pointing)
          That way, but--

Copper takes off.

                    MOTHER
          --please don't hurt him! He doesn't
          mean it! It's his condition!

Turning the corner, Copper spots the SON. Broken bottle
in hand. Stumbling. Copper chases, calling out to him. No
avail.

                    SON
          Too... it's too loud... can't...

EXT. ABANDONED BUILDING- DAY

Run down. Windows boarded. The Son runs in. Copper
catches up, stopping at the dark entrance. Contemplates.
No idea what's inside, he pulls his radio, and:

                    COPPER COLT
          Dispatch, 55-Charlie requesting
          backup. Abandoned building on 11th
          and Ocean.

INT. SQUAD CAR- DAY

Our two cops from before, Veteran and Rookie. They get the
call on the radio.

                    DISPATCH
          All available units: 55-Charlie
          requesting backup. Abandoned
          building on 11th and Ocean.

Rookie reaches for the radio on the dash. Veteran stops
him.

                    VETERAN COP
          Nuh-uh. Guy's dirty. Let God sort that
          out.

EXT. ABANDONED BUILDING- DAY

Copper paces.

                    DISPATCH
          Sorry, 55-Charlie, I'm not seeing any
          available units in the area.

                    COPPER COLT
          Stevenson walks this beat-- get him on
          the horn.

EXT. STREETS- DAY

STEVENSON waits on line at a food truck. Reading the
paper.

                    DISPATCH
          55-David, 55-Charlie has requested
          backup.

                    STEVENSON
                    (scoffs)
          Sayonara, snitch.

EXT. ABANDONED BUILDING- DAY

                    DISPATCH
          Sorry, detective. Still no units in
          your area.

Copper knows what's happening. Knows why. He takes a
moment. Pulls his sidearm. Enters alone.

INT. ABANDONED BUILDING- DAY

Dark. Dusty. Streaks of sunlight, few and far between.

Copper makes his way through. Gun at his side, pointed
downward. He presses forward. Slowly. Carefully, when--

WHAM! A 2x4 cracks him in the back of the head. He crashes
to the floor. The Son falls on top of him, and they
struggle for the gun.

                    SON
          It's too loud! Can't get away!
          Everything, everyone!

The Son has the weapon to Copper's chest. Fingers
scrambling for the trigger. Copper manages the barrel up
to the Son's neck.

No time to waste. Now or never.

Colt drops the hammer-- klik! Ready to fire. And--

POW! Belts him with a swift punch instead.

The Son falls onto Copper's chest. Asleep.

Copper lies breathless. Releases the gun's hammer, and holsters it. Grateful to not have used it.

EXT. ABANDONED BUILDING– DAY

LATER. Copper, ice pack to his head, leans against the building. Watches as a PARAMEDIC loads the Son into the ambulance. His Father and Mother join.

The Paramedic looks back at Copper to assist. He waves her off: "I'm fine".

Backup still hasn't arrived. The ambulance closes and drives off. Copper sighs. Checks the back of his head and walks off. Tossing the ice pack.

EXT. PARK– DAY

STICKY PALMER sits on a bench, siping his coffee, bouncing his knee. Passersby notice him, and he flips up his hood, hiding his face. Copper takes a seat next to him.

                    STICKY PALMER
          Not too smart for you to be seen with
          me.

                    COPPER COLT
          I don't care about all that.

                    STICKY PALMER
          Well, you should. Lawyer called. Gonna
          have to do time.

Copper knew this was going to happen. Doesn't make this any easier to swallow. Sticky shrugs. Tries to stay light.

                    STICKY PALMER
          Hey. Guess if you're gonna bump off a
          drug dealer, you'd better not be on

duty. Or get caught with your hands in
his pockets.
>   (beat; scoffs)
> All of this to try and pay a couple
> bills... only for the same bills to come
> back a month later.

Copper searches for the words.

>   COPPER COLT
> Sticky, I'm sor--

>   STICKY PALMER
> Naw, naw, don't... don't do that. You did
> the right thing. It was wrong to ask
> you to lie. Worked so hard to keep you
> clean, and when the whole thing went
> belly up, first thing I did was try and
> pull you in to cover me. Now, everyone
> either thinks you're just as dirty as
> me... or thinks you're a rat for not
> backing me up.

Sticky sips his coffee. Reflective.

>   STICKY PALMER
> Twenty years on the job, never once
> fired my weapon. First time I do... I
> waste it. Waste it on a punk. Waste it on
> his money.
>   (beat)
> Your first bullet's special, Copper.
> Can't share that with just anyone...

Copper has nothing to say. They sit there. Silent.

EXT. ROACH MOTEL- DAY

NO VACANCY. On the sign, a cartoon roach with a smile,
saying: "WE RECOMMEND IT!"

INT. ROACH MOTEL- BATHROOM- DAY

AMBROSE jerks awake as the shower turns on above him.
He's unhealthily thin. Dark circles the size of dirty
nickels under his eyes. Through the water streaming down
his face, he manages to see:

TOMMY GAT. All muscle, no brains.

> TOMMY GAT
> Don't act so surprised, kiddo. You saw
> this comin' months ago.

Ambrose looks behind Tommy. Sees a sweaty, heavyset,
well-suited man sitting on the toilet cover. Silent. A
heavy hitter. S.T. VALENTINE.

> TOMMY GAT
> How many times, huh? How many times we
> begged you to get cleaned up? Sent you
> to rehab, told you to get offa that
> stuff? You rather be a degenerate?
> Rather kill yourself with that
> garbage?

> AMBROSE
> Garbage?
> (to S.T. Valentine)
> YOU sell it.

Tommy SLAPS him upside the head.

> TOMMY GAT
> What'sa matter with you, talkin' to him
> like that? You don't wanna respect
> yourself, fine, you make sure you
> respect him. You're KILLIN' him.

> AMBROSE
> It's MY life. I do what I want.

> TOMMY GAT
> It ain't just your life. You ain't got
> two nickels to rub together to make a

third, and yet, you got a drug habit.
Who you think's pushin' you that crap?

Ambrose's eyes never leave S.T. Valentine's. Tommy SLAPS
him again, getting his attention back.

> TOMMY GAT
> It's the Feds, you moron! They're
> supplyin' you, makin' you dependent.
> Just so when you need it most, they cut
> you off, and make you rat on us for
> "just a lil' somethin', man, gimme a lil'
> somethin'."

> AMBROSE
> I wouldn't.

> TOMMY GAT
> You would. You will. And you almost
> did. You're a liability. Don't think we
> decided this. YOU did.

Ambrose's eyes turn to S.T. Valentine. Pleading.

> AMBROSE
> Dad...

Tommy looks over at S.T. Valentine. Awaiting
confirmation. S.T. Valentine nods. From his pocket, Tommy
pulls out a pair of BLACK GLOVES. Ambrose tenses up in
fear, and we--

                                                    CUT TO

EXT. ROACH MOTEL- DAY

Peaceful and calm in the morning light. The "NO VACANCY"
sign as it was. After a beat...

Tommy exits, peeling off his gloves. Checks the area.

Coast clear, he opens the door for S.T. Valentine. Puts him
in the back of a black car.

INT. BLACK CAR- DAY

S.T. Valentine doesn't move. He sits emotionless as
through his window, we see the "NO VACANCY" sign...

...turn to "VACANCY".

EXT. STICKY PALMER'S BROWNSTONE- NIGHT

Copper pulls up in his car. Shock and worry plastered on
his face. RED AND BLUE LIGHTS flashing everywhere.
POLICE CHATTER over radios.

As he walks over, he sees TWO PARAMEDICS wheeling out a
BODY BAG. STICKY PALMER'S WIFE walks alongside them.
Sobbing. Copper stands frozen, in disbelief.

A thin, dark-eyed, dark-suited man, with a nose like a
blade, emerges behind him: FINN DAGGER.

                    FINN DAGGER
          Sticky went ahead and shot himself.
          Right in the head. When THAT didn't
          work, he had to pull off ANOTHER SHOT.
                    (enjoying this)
          Poor schmuck. Couldn't even get his
          own suicide right.

Disgusted, Copper starts to walk off. Finn stops him.

                    FINN DAGGER
          You stink, sweetheart. Just cuz Sticky
          bought the farm, don't mean YOU'RE off
          the hook.

Finn walks off, an eager smile on his face. Leaving Copper
alone. Uncertain. Copper eyes Finn walking off into the
shadows...

...and then spots Stevenson. Across the street. Reading his
paper like always. Copper heads over. A steam engine,
slowly gaining speed, fueled by rage. Payback for not
backing him up. Chugga...chugga...chugga...

BWOOP! The SIREN of the ambulance snaps him out of his
rage. He looks on as it rolls into the night horizon.
Taking his dead partner with it.

Calmed and saddened, Copper walks off. Stevenson,
oblivious to the broken nose he was just spared, focuses
on his paper, until:

> DISPATCH
> All available units: assistance needed
> at the Springs 'n' Feathers Hotel.
> Repeat--

EXT. SPRINGS 'N' FEATHERS HOTEL- NIGHT

> DISPATCH (V.O.)
> --assistance needed at the Springs 'n'
> Feathers Hotel.

A slew of JOHNS and PROS, handcuffed and patted down by
police: including Stevenson, Veteran, and Rookie. Among
the Pros...

...is Sands Marquee. Hands cuffed, holding her clutch.
WE'RE BACK WHERE WE STARTED. Rookie checks her clutch:
lipstick, compact mirror, and a PAIR OF FLATS.

He pats her down: hair, breasts, outer thigh. Basic
procedure. He goes to check her inner thigh. RIGHT WHERE
THE REVOLVER IS...

...she locks eyes with him. A look as if he's patting down
his own mother. He stops, tail between his legs. Clears his
throat. Hands back the clutch.

> ROOKIE COP
> This one's clean!

INT. PRECINCT- BULLPEN- NIGHT

Tight space. Overstuffed file folders. OVERWEIGHT COPS.
If that weren't enough, now all the Johns and Pros are

being marched through.

CAPTAIN MORGAN storms out of his office. Taken aback.

                    CAPT. MORGAN
          Whoa, whoa, whoa-- what's this??

                    VETERAN COP
          I didn't ask for all this, Cap. Someone
          called 911. Left the line open.

                    CAPT. MORGAN
          Where am I supposed to put half these
          clowns? We're full enough as it is!

Some of the Pros wink and wave at the detectives and
officers. They know them pretty well. "Regulars", maybe?
The cops avoid eye contact.

                    VETERAN COP
          They're street girls, Cap. What's the
          worst could happen?

Sands trips the Pro in front of her. Steps to the side. Lets
someone else take the blame.

                    PRO 1
          Wanna watch where you goin'? Nearly
          ripped my heel off!

                    PRO 2
          'scuse me? Betta' turn around 'fore I
          "nearly rip off" somethin' else.

This one pushes that one. That one pushes back. All-out
riot. Some cops intervene. Others take pics with their
phones...

...and Sands slips through the fray. No one notices her as
she grabs a PAPERCLIP from a desk. Picks the cuffs around
her wrists.

INT. PRECINCT- MEN'S ROOM- NIGHT

Copper is at the sink, washing his face. Still reeling
from Sticky's suicide. He looks in the mirror, into his
wet reflection. His left thumb rubs his bare ring finger. A
heavy memory. By the time he notices the sound of HIGH-
HEELED SHOES in the men's room...

Too late. Sands has him locked in a chokehold. He tries to
break free. Can't fully reach behind his back. He fights
it... but gives in. Passes out... looking at her blurry, but
beautiful face in the mirror.

Copper crashes to the floor. Sands wets a paper towel,
quickly takes off her "Pro" makeup. Using the paperclip
she grabbed, she puts her hair into a MESSY BUN.

Sands pops the hem of her dress. Making it longer, closer
to the knees. PROFESSIONAL LENGTH. She takes the flats
from her clutch, and changes into them. Grabs COPPER'S
BADGE from his belt, and as she heads for the door...

...she dumps her red-bottom heels in the trash.

INT. PRECINCT- BULLPEN- NIGHT

The Pros' fight still goes on. Cops barely have a handle on
it. Sands grabs a PACK OF GUM from one desk. A TWEED
BLAZER from the back of a chair. Throws it on, rolls up the
sleeves.

She clips Copper's badge to the lapel. Pops in a stick of
gum.

INT. PRECINCT- EVIDENCE LOCKER- NIGHT

Sands enters. Tweed blazer, chewing gum, Copper's badge
and her strut... she looks, acts, breathes LIKE A COP. She
walks up to the EVIDENCE CLERK that's protected by wire
gate.

                    EVIDENCE CLERK
        Case number?

INT. PRECINCT- MEN'S ROOM- NIGHT

Copper quickly wakes up. Immediately, he checks for his
gun. Relief is short lived when he notices his badge is
missing. He runs out.

EXT. PRECINCT- NIGHT

Sands walks on her way. An EVIDENCE BOX tucked under her
arm. Copper exits. Spots her down the street, and runs.

                    COPPER COLT
        Hey! Hold it!

Sands keeps moving.

Copper presses forward. Nearing her.

Sands hikes up her dress. Reaching for her inner thigh.

Copper closes the gap between them, and--

BLAM! Sands shoots him square in the chest. Knocking him
on his back. Gasping. Raspy.

Sands walks over. Kneels beside him, placing the evidence
box down. Copper gets a good look at it:

HOMICIDE-- HART, REDD

Copper struggles to breathe. Eyes tearing up. Sands
touches his cheek, and immediately...

...his pain goes away.

                    SANDS MARQUEE
        ...shhh...

They lock eyes. Connecting. Reading.

                        160

                              SANDS MARQUEE
                       Here's your copper... Copper.

She clips the badge back on his waist. Picks up the
evidence box, and walks off.

Copper watches the healthy, lush, hourglass body walk
across the street. Sands disappears into the night
horizon, as we...

                                                      FADE OUT

INT. HOSPITAL- NIGHT

Copper sits on the bed. Shirtless. A black and blue BRUISE
right in the middle of his chest. His shirt and KEVLAR
VEST on the chair next to him.

Capt. Morgan enters.

                              CAPT. MORGAN
                   Smack dab in the vest. Nice shot, huh?

Copper cuts him a look. Not in the mood for jokes.

                              CAPT. MORGAN
                   Alright. What happened? A to Z.

Copper looks down at the badge on his belt. He considers...
and then:

                              COPPER COLT
                   The, uh... the fight with the Pros.
                   Didn't wanna have to deal with it, so I
                   went outside for a while. Saw this dame
                   walk by, tried to talk to her.

                              CAPT. MORGAN
                   You tried to talk to her... and she SHOT
                   you?

                                   161

                    COPPER COLT
          In hindsight, I coulda used a different
          set of words.

                    CAPT. MORGAN
          Ya think? What was in the box?

                    COPPER COLT
          The what?

                    CAPT. MORGAN
          The box. Under her arm. What was in
          it-- you get a look?

                    COPPER COLT
          Nah. Wasn't too focused on the
          cardboard. You know what I mean.

Capt. Morgan holds up his wedding ring.

                    CAPT. MORGAN
          Been a while since I knew what
          ANYthing meant.

Copper can't look at the jewelry. Capt. Morgan
understands.

                    CAPT. MORGAN
          .38 bullet aside, I'm proud of you.
          Talking to girls. Been a while since...

He trails off. Decides it's none of his business. After a
beat:

                    COPPER COLT
          You find her? The girl.

                    CAPT. MORGAN
          Security cam wasn't good enough. Too
          dark to get a good look at her face.
          Cheap thing, don't know why we have it,
          really.

>   (beat)
>   This ain't gonna go over well with the
>   sharks, you know.

>   COPPER COLT
>   I'm not worried about Finn Dagger.

>   CAPT. MORGAN
>   You should be. Guys in Internal Affairs
>   aren't like us. They're not scalpels.
>   They're shotguns. May have been aiming
>   for Sticky, but once they pull that
>   trigger, EVERYBODY'S taking a bullet.
>   Keep your head down, kiddo. Play
>   things smart.

Copper nods. Capt. Morgan heads for the door... but stops.

>   CAPT. MORGAN
>   She handed you something.

>   COPPER COLT
>   What?

>   CAPT. MORGAN
>   The skirt. Couldn't make out her face
>   or the box, but we think she handed you
>   something. You remember?

Beat. Copper eyes his badge.

>   COPPER COLT
>   Nope. Don't think she did.

Capt. Morgan thinks on it for a second. Finally, heads out.

>   CAPT. MORGAN
>   Rest up, Copper.

The door closes. Copper lays down on the bed, staring at
the ceiling. Chest throbbing with pain. He does what he
can. Touches his right cheek. Right where Sands touched
him. He can almost hear her voice. Soothing. Comforting.
Taking away the pain.

"shhh…"

He closes his eyes. Immersing himself in that touch, and we…

                                                    FADE OUT

INT. GREEZY SPOON DINER- DAY

THE NEXT DAY. Busy. Customers left and right, waiting for food or a seat. Sitting at the counter is MACK N. TOSH: a lanky fellow, with thick curly hair and round glasses. The WAITER walks up to him.

                    MACK N. TOSH
          Small joe. Blueberry muffin.

Copper takes a seat at the counter. Right next to Mack.

                    COPPER COLT
          Make that two muffins.

Mack takes one look at Copper, and…

                    MACK N. TOSH
          What do you want?

                    COPPER COLT
          I want you to have a big breakfast.

                    MACK N. TOSH
          Two muffins is too much for me.

                    COPPER COLT
          Okay then, I'll have it. We can eat
          together.

                    MACK N. TOSH
          What do you want?

                    COPPER COLT
          I hear it's the most important meal of
          the day.

                    (to Waiter)
            Two joes. Two muffins. On me.

The Waiter walks off. Copper and Mack sit in silence
amidst the bustling crowd of customers. Then:

                    COPPER COLT
            How've you been, Mack?

                    MACK N. TOSH
            Until you showed up? Look, whatever it
            is, it's obviously too big to wait 'til I
            get to the station, which means it's big
            enough to spoil my muffin and joe. So,
            before it gets here: What do you want?

Copper takes off his badge. Places it on the counter. Mack
puts 2 and 2 together immediately.

                    MACK N. TOSH
            How long?

                    COPPER COLT
            Soon as possible.

                    MACK N. TOSH
            No, how long was someone posing as
            police-- posing as you?

                    COPPER COLT
            Five, eight minutes. Tops. She gave it
            right back.

                    MACK N. TOSH
            She? Jesus, first a dame shoots you,
            then another one takes your...

Mack realizes. IT'S THE SAME WOMAN. Copper just looks at
him. Neither confirm nor deny.

                    MACK N. TOSH
            Jesus... You tell anyone?

                    COPPER COLT
        Tell 'em I let someone walk off with my
        BADGE? Yeah. Sent a memo.

                    MACK N. TOSH
        What're you doing to me, man? That
        whole thing with Sticky... you're
        radioactive, you know that?

The look on Copper's face. A plea for help. Mack sighs. Uses
his napkin to take the badge. Puts it in his pocket,
wrapped.

                    COPPER COLT
            I owe you one.

Their muffins and joes come. They eat in silence.

INT. PRECINCT- BULLPEN- DAY

Copper enters. Cops and detectives look at him side-eyed
as he makes his way through. He passes by a DISGRUNTLED
DETECTIVE, who, under his breath:

                    DISGRUNTLED DETECTIVE
            ...broad shoulda plugged one in yer
            ear...

Copper sits at his desk. Reads the paper already there for
him. On the front page, is a PHOTO OF S.T. VALENTINE. The
headline:

"S.T. VALENTINE QUESTIONED IN SON'S MURDER"

Across from him is an empty desk with the nameplate: DET.
SGT. STICKY PALMER. He pauses at the memory. As he starts
his work, he looks across the room...

...and sees Finn Dagger in the Captain's office. Capt.
Morgan is saying something we can't hear, but Finn is not
interested. Finn is posted by the window. Looking
straight at Copper. Not even hiding it.

Capt. Morgan notices the eye contact between Finn and Copper. He lowers the Venetian blinds, but Finn's eyes are visible between the blinds. Peering into Copper's soul.

Copper's desk phone rings. He answers.

>   MACK N. TOSH (OVER PHONE)
>   Sands Marquee.

INT. PRECINCT- FORENSICS- DAY

Copper and Mack look at a PROFESSIONAL PHOTO OF SANDS on the computer screen.

>   COPPER COLT
>   You pulled her prints. Heckuva
>   mugshot.

>   MACK N. TOSH
>   Not a mugshot. Employment file.

>   COPPER COLT
>   She's a COP?

>   MACK N. TOSH
>   File clerk. Not here-- the station over
>   on 6th. They ran her prints for a
>   background check, which put her in the
>   system.

>   COPPER COLT
>   Address?

>   MACK N. TOSH
>   (pointing to screen)
>   Ritzy part of town.

Copper jots it down on a Post-It.

>   COPPER COLT
>   You, Mr. Tosh, are an officer and a
>   gentleman.

MACK N. TOSH
What'd'ya know? Copper Colt told a joke.

Mack hands Copper back his badge. Copper tussles Mack's hair with a smile. Hurries off.

MACK N. TOSH
You still owe me one!

EXT. RITZY APARTMENT BUILDING- DAY

High-rise. Well-trimmed front yard. Tweeting birds. Silent traffic. Copper walks over. The DOORMAN lets him in.

INT. RITZY APARTMENT BUILDING- LOBBY- DAY

Copper scans the tenants' directory. Doesn't see Sands' name.

EXT. RITZY APARTMENT BUILDING- DAY

Copper heads back for the Doorman. Shows his badge.

COPPER COLT
'scuse me. Looking for a tenant here.
Sands Marquee?

DOORMAN
Can't say I know her.

COPPER COLT
Dark hair. Classy. Real high-maintenance.

DOORMAN
Ah. The five-alarm fire in six-inch heels?

COPPER COLT
That's the one.

                    DOORMAN
          Yeah, I remember her. Moved a while
          back. Gets her mail forwarded.

                   COPPER COLT
          Where?

EXT. SANDS' APARTMENT BUILDING- NIGHT

THE SLUMS. Far, far, far from the other side of town.
Copper pulls up to see: THUGS on the corner. HOMELESS
WOMEN and CHILDREN on the street.

He spots Sands walking past with groceries. Slinks in his
seat, laying low. Sands passes TWO THUGS. The first eyes
her with a smile. Opens his mouth to say something, but
the second thug nudges him.

                    THUG 2
          Nah, boy. She don't play that.

                    THUG 1
          Please. I could take her.

                    THUG 2
          Yeah, that's what Big Mike said.

                    THUG 1
          What she do to Big Mike?

                    THUG 2
          Made 'im small.

Copper eyes Sands as she enters the building.

INT. SANDS' APARTMENT- LIVING ROOM- NIGHT

She enters. Places her groceries down. Takes off her shoes,
unzips her dress.

INT. SANDS' APARTMENT— BATHROOM— NIGHT

She stands under the shower, tired and weighted. She hugs
herself. As if her arms were someone else's, and we...

                                              DISSOLVE TO

INT. RITZY APARTMENT BUILDING— LIVING ROOM— DAY
(FLASHBACK)

Sands stands much BRIGHTER and HAPPIER than we're
accustomed. A PAIR OF HANDS over her eyes. Behind her is a
casually, yet smartly, dressed man. Drop dead gorgeous.
REDD HART.

                    REDD HART
           Okay... and... open.

He removes his hands, revealing the beautiful living
room to Sands. She beams.

                    SANDS MARQUEE
           Oh, my God... this is...

                    REDD HART
           Pretty swell, huh?

He takes Sands into his arms. Dances with her across the
room.

                    REDD HART
           Roomy. Inviting. Great for guests and
           parties...

He twirls her onto the couch.

                    REDD HART
           ...yet, perfect for late night
           conversations with Chinese takeout
           and wine for two.

He pulls her back up.

KITCHEN. Dips her in so she can take a look.

> REDD HART
> Fully set up. Everything state of the
> art.

BATHROOM. Twirls her inside.

> REDD HART
> The only leaky plumbing in the
> apartment is... well, YOUR leaky
> plumbing.

Sands laughs.

BEDROOM. They waltz inside, ending with a flourish.

> REDD HART
> Now, the bedroom... there's a small
> draft, so it could get a bit chilly in
> the winter. But, that shouldn't be a
> problem at all... with the right
> company.

He pulls her close. His hands explore. Lips against her
neck. She giggles.

> SANDS MARQUEE
> You can't sell an apartment you've
> already "broken in", that's horrible.

> REDD HART
> Sell? Sands, babe... it's bought.

Sands pulls away from Redd. Shocked.

> SANDS MARQUEE
> ...I can't live here.

> REDD HART
> You have to.

> SANDS MARQUEE
> Are you crazy? This is too big!

                    REDD HART
            Exactly. It's too much without you.

From his breast pocket, Redd pulls out a sheet of paper:
Rolled up, tied with YARN. He shows her. It's the LEASE.

                  SANDS MARQUEE
            ...you're crazy, you know that?

                    REDD HART
            Wait for it...

He rolls the paper again, slips the yarn around it... and
gets down on one knee. Ties the other end of the yarn
around her ring finger. Sands holds back her tears.
Dumbfounded. Words escape.

Redd looks up at her. A debonair smile that could melt.

                    REDD HART
            Don't worry. It's only 'til forever.

Sands kneels down as well. Goes to kiss him, but we--

                                        SMASH CUT TO

INT. SANDS' APARTMENT- LIVING ROOM- NIGHT

PRESENT DAY. Sands stands in her robe. In her tiny, creaky
apartment. Alone with her memory. The stolen EVIDENCE
BOX on the coffee table. From the box, she pulls out an
evidence bag with a YARN BRACELET inside. The same yarn
that was once tied around her finger.

She tears up.

EXT. SANDS' APARTMENT BUILDING- NIGHT

Copper is still in his car. Keeping watch. Sees a YOUNG
COUPLE come around the corner. They don't belong in this
side of town. As they pass by the two thugs from before, the
Young Man holds the Young Woman close.

                        172

                    YOUNG MAN
            Don't worry. I'm right here...

Copper misses that. That connection. That loyalty. That
love. As he watches the young couple pass, his left thumb
rubs against his bare ring ringer.

Right in front of the car, Tommy Gat and TWO GOOMBAHS
pass. Heading straight for Sands' apartment building.
They enter. Recognizing them, Copper grabs his radio:

                    COPPER
            55-David requesting...

He remembers how well that worked last time. Hangs up.
Quickly gets out and heads for the building.

INT. SANDS' APARTMENT BUILDING- LOBBY- NIGHT

Tommy and the two Goombahs enter the elevator. Copper
takes the stairs.

INT. SANDS' APARTMENT- LIVING ROOM- NIGHT

Still in nothing but her robe, Sands puts the yarn around
her wrist. Reminiscing. She then pulls out a WALLET from
the evidence box. Goes through it. Inside, is a KEY with
its head in the SHAPE OF A STAR.

A KNOCK on the door. Far from frightened, she knows who it
is. Puts the wallet on the far side of the coffee table.
Leaves the box right where it is.

She opens the door, revealing Tommy and the Goombahs.

                    TOMMY GAT
            Boss wants to see ya.

                    SANDS MARQUEE
            I'm not dressed.

TOMMY GAT
(greasy smile)
Then he'll REALLY wanna see ya.

Sands steps aside as Goombah 1 enters, and grabs the
evidence box. Oblivious to the wallet on the other side of
the coffee table. Sands leaves with them.

INT. SANDS' APARTMENT BUILDING- HALLWAY- NIGHT

As Copper peeps around the corner, Sands, Tommy and the
two Goombahs enter the elevator.

With a groan, Copper heads back down the stairs.

EXT. STREETS- NIGHT

A BLACK CAR rolls past.

INT. BLACK CAR- NIGHT

Goombah 1 sits behind the wheel. The evidence box in the
front passenger seat. Sands is in the back. Tommy and
Goombah 2 sit on either side of her.

Tommy casually rests his hand on Sands' thigh. Much too
close for comfort. She glares down at it.

TOMMY GAT
No worries, doll face. Be there in just
a sec.

Sands bites her tongue. Focuses straight ahead. Through
the back window, we see Copper's car trailing behind them.

INT. COPPER'S CAR- NIGHT

Copper keeps a safe distance. Hands tight on the wheel.
Ready.

EXT. THE JOINT- NIGHT

The black car pulls up. Tommy steps out first, offers his
hand to assist Sands out as well.

She gets out on her own. Tommy can't help but smile.

INT. THE JOINT- NIGHT

A CROONER onstage, softly singing. Tommy, Sands and the
two Goombahs walk through. All eyes, mostly male, fall on
Sands, who wears nothing but a robe. She doesn't bother
with their ogles.

They make their way to a booth. S.T. Valentine sits by
himself, eating. Silent. Lost in thought.

Copper trails far behind. Takes a seat at the far end of the
bar. Keeps a corner eye on Sands.

                    SANDS MARQUEE
          How's your boy?

                    S.T. VALENTINE
          Never you mind. Any progress?

                    SANDS MARQUEE
          Some.

                    S.T. VALENTINE
          Don't play games, girlie. Come clean.

                    SANDS MARQUEE
          I told you, this is something that
          would take time.

                    S.T. VALENTINE
          You got the box.

                    SANDS MARQUEE
          Didn't have much time to see what's IN
          the box.

                    S.T. VALENTINE
          You got it LAST NIGHT. Just about 24
          hours to read through it.

                    SANDS MARQUEE
          I'm dyslexic.

Valentine SNAPS his fingers, and-- THWAP!-- Tommy SLAPS
her. Everything stops. Music, singing, chatter. All eyes
look on.

Copper takes the latch off his gun holster. Edges closer.

                    S.T. VALENTINE
          Redd was smart. Clever. You? You're just
          the broad he slept with. You wanna
          start gettin' ideas? DON'T.

The music slowly resumes. The Crooner goes back to
singing.

                    S.T. VALENTINE
          Where's my dope?

                    SANDS MARQUEE
          I don't know.

                    S.T. VALENTINE
          When WILL you know?

                    SANDS MARQUEE
          This isn't something I can rush.

TWO SNAPS. Tommy kicks Sands' chair out from under her.
She grabs hold of the tablecloth, bringing plates and
glasses down with her. They SHATTER. The music stops.

Copper gets up to intervene. A CIGAR GIRL gets in the way.

                    CIGAR GIRL
          What's your pleasure, sugar?

Valentine dabs his mouth with his napkin.

176

                    S.T. VALENTINE
          Three snaps, and...

Tommy puts his hand on the back of his belt, ready to pull.
He grabs a fistful of Sands' hair. She BREAKS DOWN. Tears
flowing like a poorly built dam.

                    SANDS MARQUEE
          I DON'T KNOW! You've got me lying,
          stealing, the cops on my back...! I
          wasn't made for this! This isn't the
          kinda job for a woman-- not the kinda
          life for a woman to have!

Valentine cleans his teeth. Unbothered.

                    SANDS MARQUEE
          I'm not made for this. I need time.
          Please, I... I need time.

Valentine gestures over a couple of BUS BOYS.

                    S.T. VALENTINE
          One more day.

The Bus Boys pick up the shattered dishes. Valentine
returns his attention to Sands, still on the floor.

                    S.T. VALENTINE
          Tick-tock, girlie.

Sands rises, still tearing. Makes the long walk of shame
back to the exit. As soon as all eyes are behind her, all
eyes except for Copper... her demeanor changes. No longer
sobbing. Her face is hard. Cold. Dead.

It was all an act. And Copper realizes as the music resumes
once more.

INT. SANDS' APARTMENT- LIVING ROOM- NIGHT

She enters. Heads straight for her mini-bar. Pours herself
a glass of Jack. Just as she nears it to her lips... a KNOCK

                          177

at the door.

Annoyed, she opens. Sees Copper. They eye each other for a long, pregnant beat, and:

>   SANDS MARQUEE
>   Speedy recovery.

She steps aside. Copper enters.

>   SANDS MARQUEE
>   Drink?

>   COPPER COLT
>   I don't touch the stuff.

>   SANDS MARQUEE
>   Wuss.

She takes a seat on the couch. Copper stands there, badge illuminating in what little light there is at night. He eyes her. Irked.

>   SANDS MARQUEE
>   I felt your vest when I knocked you
>   out. Knew the bullet wouldn't go
>   through.

>   COPPER COLT
>   Kevlar isn't THAT reliable. You
>   could've easily killed me.

She sips her Jack.

>   SANDS MARQUEE
>   You're welcome.

>   COPPER COLT
>   Don't do that. Don't play hardball with
>   me. Not when you've got scum like
>   Tommy Gat and S.T. Valentine for
>   playdates. What're you doing hanging
>   around those guys-- don't you read the
>   papers? The man killed his own son.

                    SANDS MARQUEE
        ...He what?

                    COPPER COLT
        Yeah. Killed his own son. Probably to
        keep his crew clean from the Feds.

Sands has a hard time swallowing this.

                    SANDS MARQUEE
        He loves his son.

                    COPPER COLT
        S.T. Valentine loves himself. His
        power, his money, his business.

Sands sits in deep thought. Finishes her drink. Copper
takes a seat next to her on the couch.

                    COPPER COLT
        What do they want with you?

Something about his eyes... They make her uncomfortable.
Something she hasn't felt in a while.

                    SANDS MARQUEE
        They... they asked me to break into
        your station. Steal an evidence box.

                    COPPER COLT
        Why you?

                    SANDS MARQUEE
        Why not?

                    COPPER COLT
        You for hire?

                    SANDS MARQUEE
        Everyone is.

                    COPPER COLT
        Girl like you-- what's your rate?

                         179

                    SANDS MARQUEE
          More than you can afford.

She heads over to the mini-bar. Refills.

                    COPPER COLT
          What's so important about the box?
          Who's Redd Hart?

                    SANDS MARQUEE
          S.T. Valentine and Tommy Gat may be
          dangerous, but them? Them, I know.
          You...?

Copper nears.

                    COPPER COLT
          I don't screw people over. I'm police.

                    SANDS MARQUEE
          Ha. Detective Moron. Detective Oxy
          Moron.

                    COPPER COLT
          I'm not like the rest.

                    SANDS MARQUEE
          Said every Dick ever.

Copper takes the drink from her. Slams it back on the
mini-bar. It spills.

                    COPPER COLT
          Look. If I wanted to send you up the
          river, I'd've done it faster than the
          speeding bullet you kissed me with.

                    SANDS MARQUEE
          Why don't you?

                    COPPER COLT
          Because I want to help.

                    SANDS MARQUEE
          Single-handedly broke into your
          precinct, took down a man twice my
          size-- that was YOU, by the way-- and
          helped your friends get the biggest
          number of arrests in one night. I don't
          need, or want your help, but for the
          arrests, I will accept a "thank you".

                    COPPER COLT
          What'sa matter with you? You know, for
          someone with all those looks, it'd be
          nice if you had some brains to go with
          it.

                    SANDS MARQUEE
          Excuse me?

                    COPPER COLT
          S.T. Valentine's got enough cronies to
          do his dirty work for him-- what
          kinda outside idiot wakes up one day
          and DECIDES to help him out?

Sands steps in Copper's face.

                    SANDS MARQUEE
          I am NOT your average idiot.

Copper doesn't back down. In fact, he leans in. As if he's
reading her:

                    COPPER COLT
             No. No, you're not, are you?

They stand face to face. She starts to turn away, but his
massive hands gently take her by the arms. Keeping her in
place. Making her look at him. Her hand goes against his
chest as she tries to step back.

                    SANDS MARQUEE
             What're you doing?

                    COPPER COLT
          I want you to see me.

                    SANDS MARQUEE
          For what?

                    COPPER COLT
          For who I am.

Her hand on his chest cups his heart. She looks into his
eyes. His hands let her go, but his eyes don't. Those pained
wounded eyes. They stare for a moment, until his eyes
shift, and he realizes...

...the WALLET on the coffee table. He walks over to it.

                    COPPER COLT
          You don't seem the type for men's
          wallets. This was in the box? You just
          laid it out on the table?

                    SANDS MARQUEE
          No need to hide it. Nothing's more
          hidden than the obvious.

Copper gives her a look. Unconvinced.

                    SANDS MARQUEE
          Say you rob a bank. Cops are coming,
          time to make your getaway. Where do
          you go? Next county? Next city?

                    COPPER COLT
          You tell me.

                    SANDS MARQUEE
          You go across the street. No one EVER
          looks right in front of them.

                    COPPER COLT
          Glasses on your face, and all that.

Copper looks the wallet over. Notices the STAR-HEADED
key inside.

                    COPPER COLT
        What's this?

                    SANDS MARQUEE
        No idea.

He goes through the wallet. Sees the cash inside. Sands
walks over to the bathroom, undoing her robe.

                    SANDS MARQUEE
        I'm going to get undressed, detective.

Just as the robe drops, she disappears around the corner.
Copper quickly turns away. Uncomfortable.

                    SANDS MARQUEE (O.S.)
        If you're as different as you say, you'll
        close the door on your way out.

Copper's hurt from being sent off so abruptly. He hides it.
Regarding the wallet:

                    COPPER COLT
        I'll be taking this with me.

                    SANDS MARQUEE (O.S)
        I look like I need the money?

Copper looks at the dingy apartment. She does, actually.
He pockets the wallet and takes his leave. Closing the
door behind him. After a beat...

...Sands steps out of the bathroom. Looks at the closed
door. Thinking. Wondering.

EXT. SANDS' APARTMENT BUILDING— NIGHT

Copper exits to see Finn Dagger leaning on his car.

                    FINN DAGGER
        Not your jurisdiction, detective.
        Moonlighting?

                        183

                    COPPER COLT
          Haven't you heard? I'm one of those
          superheroes. Long underwear, and
          everything.

INT. COPPER'S CAR- NIGHT

Copper gets in. So does Finn.

                    COPPER COLT
               Look, I--

                    FINN DAGGER
          Probably hungry. I know a place.

                    COPPER COLT
               It's late.

On the clock: 2AM.

                    FINN DAGGER
          You kidding? It's morning. Come on.
          You'll love it.

With no choice, Copper drives off.

INT. GREEZY SPOON DINER- NIGHT

It's late. Not many patrons or employees. Copper and Finn
sit at the counter. Copper works on a coffee. Finn enjoys a
full breakfast: French Toast, bacon, and runny eggs.

Awkward silence. Filled with nothing but the sounds of
Finn's fork and knife. After a beat:

                    COPPER COLT
          You plan on making a move, or you
          gonna keep playing footsie all night?

                    FINN DAGGER
          Slow down, detective. You gotta EARN
          the cigarette afterwards. Besides,

what'd Ol' Blue Eyes say? "Nice 'n' easy
does it every time".

Finn finishes his plate. Hands it back to the WAITRESS
with a wink. He turns to Copper, cleaning his teeth with a
smile. Still saying nothing.

                    COPPER COLT
          Sticky's dead. Let it go.

                    FINN DAGGER
          Oh, I already got Sticky. He confessed.
          That's why he swallowed a bullet.
          Couldn't stomach jail time. But, you...
          He loved you, didn't he? Like a son.

                    COPPER COLT
          Whatever he did was on him. I wasn't
          involved.

                    FINN DAGGER
          Really? All his dirt, his crimes, his
          cover ups... that all happened without
          your knowledge?

                    COPPER COLT
          He kept it hidden.

                    FINN DAGGER
          Horsecrap. Sticky was such a screw-up,
          he had to call "do-over" on his own
          suicide, for Chrissake. You helping
          him pull jobs for S.T. Valentine makes
          more sense than two and two making
          four.

                    COPPER COLT
          You get off on this, don't you? Witch
          hunts. Burning cops at the stake.

                    FINN DAGGER
          Sticky was NOT a cop. He was DIRTY.

185

                    COPPER COLT
         And you're a rat. And I don't have to
         listen to this.

                    FINN DAGGER
         Truth hurts, don't it, sweetheart?

                    COPPER COLT
         I'd offer you a ride home, but you're
         just about the ugliest dame I ever met.

Copper starts to leave, but--

                    FINN DAGGER
         Still a virgin, ain'tcha?

He stops in his tracks.

                    FINN DAGGER
         Yeah, you are. Read your jacket. Bum
         town like this, and you ain't pulled
         the trigger yet. Then again, it took
         Sticky twenty years to fire his weapon.
         And when he did, it was cuz he was
         crooked. And when YOU do... when you
         pull that trigger, when you take
         another man's life, you're gonna do it
         for the same reason Sticky did: for
         your own filthy, self-interest. And I'm
         gonna be there. I'm gonna be the guy
         who puts the bracelets on you. I'm
         gonna be the "rat" who locks you up
         with all the other scumbags YOU locked
         up-- every last one of 'em just itching
         to walk up to you in your sleep to say
         "SHANK you very much".

Copper is frozen for a beat. Weighted with the outlook of
his future. He walks off. Leaving Finn with his coffee.
And his smile.

INT. COPPER'S APARTMENT- LIVING ROOM- NIGHT

Copper enters. Tired. He schleps through, taking off his
tie, unbuttoning his shirt. Realizes his badge isn't on
his waist.

FLASHBACK: Sands' Apartment. Copper grabs Sands. Pulls
her close. She lifts his badge.

Copper smiles to himself.

                    COPPER COLT
          Heh. Fastest hands in the west.

INT. COPPER'S APARTMENT- BATHROOM- NIGHT

He showers. Not as dead as before. Lighter. A HAPPIER
thought on his mind, as we...

                                        DISSOLVE TO

INT. BROWNSTONE- DAY (FLASHBACK)

Empty. Even without furnishings, it has warmth. A HOME in
every sense.

The door opens. BRIGHT SUNLIGHT bleeds in, wrapping
around the TWO FIGURES in the door frame: One of whom is
Copper, marvelously dressed, and...

...ARIAL BLACK. A truly beautiful and enchanting sight. A
small town girl. New city, new home, new love. She's
breathless at the sight of the house.

                    ARIAL BLACK
          Oh, my God...

                    COPPER COLT
          S'all ours, baby.

                    ARIAL BLACK
              Never in my life have I...

Completely taken over, she runs to Copper, who takes her
in his arms. Spins her around. They laugh. Elated.

KITCHEN. Taking her by the hand, Copper leads her
through.

                    COPPER COLT
              Just imagine: Sunday morning
              breakfast. Bacon sizzling, music
              playing, all five kids laughing...

                    ARIAL BLACK
              Five? Can we afford to adopt four other
              kids?

                    COPPER COLT
              Nuh-uh. Spawn of my loins, baby.

                    ARIAL BLACK
              I am NOT giving birth five times.

                    COPPER COLT
              No worries. The first four are two sets
              of twins, and--

                    ARIAL BLACK
              You're evil.

                    COPPER COLT
              Alright, then, it's settled. We convert
              to Mormonism, and--

                    ARIAL BLACK
              Shut up.

They laugh. He lifts her up on the kitchen counter. Hands
mapping out her full hips and thighs. She plays with his
collar.

                    ARIAL BLACK
          Easy, big bad. Wedding's in two weeks.
          Daddy'll be mad if you eat before you
          pray.

                    COPPER COLT
          Last I checked, daddy don't matter no
          more. Last I checked, daddy just got
          replaced.

He takes Arial's hand. Kisses the ENGAGEMENT RING. He
looks into her eyes. Meaning every word:

                    COPPER COLT
          Don't you go nowhere. You hear me?

                    ARIAL BLACK
          I hear you.

They close in to kiss, and we--

                                              SMASH CUT TO

INT. COPPER'S APARTMENT- BEDROOM- NIGHT

PRESENT DAY. Copper is tossed out of the bed, the mattress
rolling over.

                    TOMMY GAT
          You think I don't know when I'm bein'
          tailed?

Copper yanks the drawer from the bedside dresser. Draws
his gun on Tommy. Pulls the trigger-- tik!

Tommy holds up the CLIP from Copper's gun.

                    TOMMY GAT
          Not my first rodeo, cowboy. Didn't see a
          badge in there, so I guess you're no
          cop. So, what, you some kinda friend of
          Redd's? The broad get you to help out?
          Put the screws to us?

                    COPPER COLT
          I don't know what you're talking about.

                    TOMMY GAT
          Where's the drugs? Where's the dough?

Copper LAUNCHES at Tommy. Tommy traps him in a hold.
SLAMS him on the floor.

                    TOMMY GAT
          She can't be trusted. We tell her to do
          one thing, and she ends up breaking
          into a cop house. She trynna screw us
          over? She think she can break free?

Copper just looks at him. Rage in his eyes.

                    TOMMY GAT
          Ah. Tough guy, huh? Let's see just HOW
          tough.

Tommy LAUNCHES his fist, and we--

                                        CUT TO BLACK

All we hear are blows LANDING. Furniture CRASHING.
Copper GRUNTING.

EXT. STREETS- NIGHT

Casually walking over to a brownstone, is MICKEY KEYS.
16. Delinquent. Heckuva brain. From his vintage Gamarra
High varsity jacket, he pulls out a LOCK-PICK SET. Gets to
work.

His cell RINGS. Loud. He hurries to shut it off. Sees who's
calling: MOMS. He answers.

                    MICKEY KEYS
          Hey, ma, what's--?

Nothing but SCREAMING and HOLLERING. She's pissed.

                         190

                    MICKEY KEYS
          WHAT, I wasn't DOIN' nothin'! I'm with T
          and them, I'm not... Alright, ALRIGHT!
          I'm COMIN'!

He puts his pick set away. Walks off, dejected.

                    MICKEY KEYS
          Jeez...

INT. MICKEY'S APARTMENT- NIGHT

Mickey enters, closing the door behind him.

                    MICKEY KEYS
          I wasn't DOIN' nothin', mom, I SWEAR. I
          was just--

Next to MAMA KEYS is Copper. BANDAGE over his nose. CUTS
and BRUISES. A FAT LIP.

                    MICKEY KEYS
          Whoa. What happened to YOU?

Copper shows Mickey the STAR KEY from Redd's wallet.

                    COPPER COLT
          What does this open?

                    MICKEY KEYS
          Man, HOW would I know? I break in ONE
          TIME, and you ALWAYS comin' up in here,
          trynna put the frame on me like I'm
          some kinda--

Mama Keys SLAPS him upside the head.

                    MAMA KEYS
          Don't you START that lyin', now!

                    MICKEY KEYS
          OKAY, okay! Star Safety Storage,
          alright? The star-- it's the head of

every key you get when you sign up for
a storage locker. Jeez...

                    COPPER COLT
          Thanks, Mick.

Copper kisses Mama Keys on the cheek.

                    COPPER COLT
          Ma'am.

                    MAMA KEYS
          Nice seeing you again, detective. You
          take care of that gorgeous face, now.

Mama Keys smiles. Copper takes his leave. Mama Keys goes
to work on Mickey.

                    MAMA KEYS
          DIDN'T. I. TELL. YOU--!

                    MICKEY KEYS
          I wasn't DOIN' nothin'! JEEZ!

INT. SANDS' APARTMENT- BEDROOM- DAY

Sands lies on the far side of the bed. The other side
untouched. Bare. She wakes. Reaches over, touching the
empty space.

INT. SANDS' APARTMENT- BATHROOM- DAY

She showers. Slowly. Methodically. Closes her eyes, lowers
her head under the water...

FLASHBACK: Redd in bed. A white bed sheet across his rosy
skin. Sands' hand reaches in to stroke his chest hair,
but--

She SNAPS OUT OF IT. Pulls her head out from under the
water. No time for memories.

                         192

INT. SANDS' APARTMENT- LIVING ROOM- DAY

Hair in a MESSY BUN. BLACK DRESS slipped on. A TWEED
JACKET over it. COPPER'S BADGE pinned to the lapel.

She loads her REVOLVER. Puts it in her clutch. Walks out
the door, closing it behind her.

EXT. STAR SAFETY STORAGE- DAY

"Cop" sunglasses on, chewing gum, Sands walks over.
Focused.

INT. STAR SAFETY STORAGE- DAY

Sands approaches the STORAGE LANDLORD. Makes sure the
badge on her lapel is in plain view.

                    SANDS MARQUEE
               Detective Colt, Homicide. I need to
               take a look at the names of renters. You
               got a list?

                    STORAGE LANDLORD
               You got a WARRANT?

She drops her revolver on the counter with a thud!

                    SANDS MARQUEE
          Six.

The Storage Landlord gulps. Hands her his book.

                    STORAGE LANDLORD
               T-take a look...

                    SANDS MARQUEE
          Take a walk.

He skitters off. Sands looks through the list of names.
Spots one:

She feels someone coming up behind her. She spins around, aiming her gun--

--at Copper. The bruises on his face... she pauses at them.

>   COPPER COLT
>   Talk.

>   SANDS MARQUEE
>   ...I told you. I'm hired for a job.

Copper moves in closer. Stares down the revolver's barrel.

>   COPPER COLT
>   These bruises? They ain't cuz I wanted
>   to look pretty. Tommy Gat stopped by.
>   From the way he was talking, Valentine
>   didn't hire you for a job, HE'S GOT THE
>   SCREWS IN YOU. Whatever it is he's got
>   on you, they're gonna pull the trigger
>   on it soon as you finish. You wanna
>   live to see another day, you'd better
>   start talking.

>   SANDS MARQUEE
>   YOU'RE gonna help ME live? Which part
>   of the GUN IN MY HAND do you not
>   understand: the trigger or the bullet?

Copper's not having it. Grabs her by the gun arm. Flips her over his back, SLAMMING her hard on top the counter. They struggle, but his weight lays across her. Irrefutable.

>   COPPER COLT
>   Redd Hart. You. S.T. Valentine and
>   Tommy Gat.

He YANKS the gun from her.

>   COPPER COLT
>   TALK.

SILENCE. After a beat... finally:

                    SANDS MARQUEE (V.O.)
          Redd Hart was a man.

INT. RITZY APARTMENT- DAY (FLASHBACK)

Redd, in just a sweatshirt and a pair of briefs, sips his
coffee by the window. A cool breeze.

                    SANDS MARQUEE (V.O.)
          Large hands, and slender arms.
          Generous shoulders to rest your heart
          on, and hair on his chest that crackled
          like fresh bread as your fingers ran
          across.

Sands comes up beside him. Hugging his waist. She wears
the YARN BRACELET and a WEDDING RING. He smiles. Kisses
her forehead.

                    SANDS MARQUEE (V.O.)
          A smile that could kill, and eyes...
          eyes of...

She looks into his eyes. Warm. Filled with light.

                    SANDS MARQUEE (V.O.)
          ...resurrection.

She rests her head on his chest. Comforted.

                    SANDS MARQUEE (V.O.)
          Redd Hart was a MAN. But more than just
          the physical sense.

ANOTHER TIME. Redd and Sands play around. Laughing like
two kids. What was supposed to be hot chocolate and
movies, has turned into a food fight. Marshmallows and
whipped cream all over.

                    SANDS MARQUEE (V.O.)
          He clothed me with his warmth. Carried
          me with his hope. Made me weak with a
          laugh, and gave me life with every
          glance.

BEDROOM. Redd in bed. A white bed sheet across his rosy
skin. Sands' hand reaches in to stroke his chest hair. He
kisses her hand as he looks at her-- at US. And we fall in
love just as well.

                    SANDS MARQUEE (V.O.)
          Redd Hart was a man. Redd Hart was MY
          man.

LIVING ROOM. Night. Redd climbs in through the open
window. Hat, shirt, gloves and jeans: all black. He thinks
the coast is clear, but sees Sands. Standing in her robe.

                    SANDS MARQUEE (V.O.)
          He was an honest man. With DISHONEST
          employment.

They argue. He tries to explain. Sands doesn't want to
hear it.

                    SANDS MARQUEE (V.O.)
          He never hurt anyone. Never stole from
          someone who couldn't do without. I
          didn't approve. At first.

She turns her back to him. Can't listen anymore. But the
mere stroke of her hair. The touch of his hand against her
shoulder. She tries to fight it.

                    SANDS MARQUEE (V.O.)
          I was scared. Terrified. But, when you
          love a man...

They embrace. Warm. Complete.

                    SANDS MARQUEE (V.O.)
          ...YOU LOVE A MAN. Faults and all.

DISSOLVE TO

Day. Close on Sands' face. Eyes closed. Slowly PULL BACK TO
REVEAL:

                    SANDS MARQUEE
          ...98...99...100.

She's all alone in the living room. Immediately, she heads
for the--

KITCHEN. Sees nothing.

BATHROOM. Nothing.

BEDROOM. Still nothing.

LIVING ROOM. She plops down on the couch. All out of
ideas. Finally:

                    SANDS MARQUEE
          Okay, I give up!
               (no response...)
          Redd...?

Redd pops out from behind the couch, startling her. She
laughs.

                    SANDS MARQUEE
          Are you kidding me?? Right here, the
          whole time??

                    REDD HART
          Tol'ja I'd win.

                    SANDS MARQUEE
          How'd you know I wouldn't look there?

                    REDD HART
          Say you rob a bank. Cops are coming,
          time to make your escape. Where do you
          go? Next county? Next city?

                    SANDS MARQUEE
          You tell me.

                    REDD HART
          You go across the street. No one ever
          looks right in front of them. Nothing's
          more hidden than the obvious.

                    SANDS MARQUEE
          Show-off.

He softly touches her face. Strokes her hair.

                    REDD HART
          Show hasn't started, yet.

He goes for a kiss, and we--

                                                    CUT TO

EXT. STREETS- DAY (FLASHBACK)

ERRKSS! A BLACK CAR screeches to a stop right in front of
Redd. The door opens.

                    S.T. VALENTINE
          Get in.

INT. BLACK CAR- DAY (FLASHBACK)

Tommy Gat drives. Redd is in the back with Valentine, who
pitches his plan.

                    SANDS MARQUEE (V.O.)
          His talents didn't go unnoticed. Soon
          enough, S.T. Valentine wanted to meet
          with him. A rival crew had a drug
          business brewing. The Feds broke it up
          and confiscated everything. Valentine
          wanted the drugs and the cash from the
          evidence warehouse. He wanted Redd to
          get it for him.

                        198

Valentine holds his hand out. Redd thinks on it. Shakes it with a smile.

EXT. WAREHOUSE- NIGHT (FLASHBACK)

In his cat burglar outfit, Redd runs off. LARGE DUFFEL BAG on his back. Accomplished.

                    SANDS MARQUEE (V.O.)
          Redd was playful. A little TOO playful.
          Steal the cash? Sell the drugs and make
          off with the whole payday? Make a FOOL
          of S.T. Valentine?

Redd runs off into the night as we FADE OUT.

                    SANDS MARQUEE (V.O.)
          He laughed about it. Laughed himself
          to DEATH.

                                        SMASH CUT TO

INT. RITZY APARTMENT- NIGHT (FLASHBACK)

BEDROOM. Redd is YANKED from the bed. SLAMMED to the floor by Tommy Gat and Goombah 1. Sands is held down in bed by Goombah 2.

                    SANDS MARQUEE
          Redd!

                    TOMMY GAT
          Shaddup, chickie!
                    (to Redd)
          Where is it?

                    REDD HART
          What're you talking abou--?

Tommy grabs Redd. CRASHES him into the dresser. Sands tries to break free. Goombah 2 uses the bed sheet as a straight jacket.

                    SANDS MARQUEE
              Leave him alone! He didn't--!

                    TOMMY GAT
              Keep that broad QUIET!
                    (to Goombah 1)
              Press 'im.

Goombah 1 SLAMS Redd to the floor again. His knee in his
chest. Tommy TRASHES the bedroom. FLIPS over the mattress
with Sands still on it, sending her CRASHING. Tommy
leaves, checking the other rooms. All we hear is the sound
of Tommy's OFF-SCREEN SEARCH AND DESTROY, as:

Both on the floor, Sands and Redd share a look. Seeing
each other from under the bed. She's terrified. Tears
streaming. Redd is calm. Soothing. He's already welcomed
the outcome.

Tommy enters. Enraged. Pulls his gun.

                    TOMMY GAT
              Get 'em up!

The Goombahs do so. Sands and Redd, separated by their
marriage bed, never take their eyes off each other.

                    TOMMY GAT
              Where is it?

                    REDD HART
              Alright, look. Just calm down. Let her
              go, and I'll--

                    TOMMY GAT
              NO. No games. No deals, you rat. YOU
              TELL ME WHERE IT--!!

Tommy GESTURES with his gun hand, and-- BLAM!

Redd's eyes open wide.

Goombah 1 lets him go. In shock, as well.

                         200

Redd falls to his knees. Then on his face.

Tommy looks at the gun in his hand. Totally unexpected.

Sands is dumbfounded. Words escape. Her eyes never leave her dead husband.

Tommy looks at Redd. Then Sands. Figures out a new approach. He makes his way over to her. MENACING, as we...

> DISSOLVE TO

INT. STAR SAFETY STORAGE- DAY

PRESENT DAY. Copper looks on as Sands recounts, sitting on the counter.

> SANDS MARQUEE
> They set me up for it. Forced the gun in my hand, got my prints on it. With the apartment trashed, it looked like a lovers' quarrel.

> COPPER COLT
> You could fight it. Prove you didn't kill him.

> SANDS MARQUEE
> Yes. That's worked SO WELL in the past. Besides, from what I hear, S.T. Valentine's got a couple cops on his payroll-- ready, willing, and waiting to charge me and cage me for an easy payday.

Copper tries to bury his memory of Sticky. Now's not the time.

> COPPER COLT
> They want the drugs and cash. If anyone knows where Redd hid it, it's you.

                    SANDS MARQUEE
          I saw the key in his wallet, and
          remembered Redd loved the doughnut
          shop near this place. If he was gonna
          stash the drugs, he'd stash them here.

                    COPPER COLT
          Find anything?

Sands shows him the renters list.

                    SANDS MARQUEE
          Here. A name on the list.

                    COPPER COLT
          "Andrew Lee Simmons"? What makes you
          so sure this is him?

                    SANDS MARQUEE
          The initials. "A.L.S." Say it fast
          enough, and it sounds like--

                    COPPER COLT
          "Alias". Unreal.

                    SANDS MARQUEE
          Nothing's more hidden than the
          obvious.

BLAM! A bullet rips through the book on the counter.
Copper quickly pulls Sands to the floor.

BLAM! BLAM! BLAM! Tommy and the two Goombahs open fire on
them.

Copper takes Sands by the hand and runs off with her.
Farther into the facility as BULLETS EXPLODE around
them.

Tommy and the two Goombahs pursue... only to see ROWS
UPON ROWS OF STORAGE LOCKERS. They split up.

Copper and Sands, kneeling in a corner somewhere:

> COPPER COLT
> Get to the locker. Stay inside.

He hands her the key. As Copper runs off, Sands pulls her gun from the back of his belt. He doesn't even feel it.

Goombah 1 sneaks down a row of lockers. Gun tight in his hand. Copper appears behind him. Puts his gun to his back. He drops the hammer-- klik!-- not saying a word.

MOMENTS LATER-- Tommy Gat turns the corner, and sees Goombah 1 CUFFED TO A PIPE.

> TOMMY GAT
> You shacked with the wrong dame, Dick!

Elsewhere, Copper makes his way through. Gun hand steady.

> TOMMY GAT (O.S.)
> If she was half as smart as she looks,
> she'd'a known there was a CHECKLIST in
> the evidence box!

Copper turns the corner. Goombah 2 RAMS INTO HIM. They struggle for each other's guns.

> TOMMY GAT (O.S.)
> Soon as we figured out the wallet was
> missing, we tailed her!

Copper's gun is knocked to the floor. He goes for the back of his belt, where Sands' gun was. Realizes it's gone.

Sands walks over to REDD'S STORAGE LOCKER. Using the key, she enters.

Copper struggles with Goombah 2. He's SLAMMED against the lockers again and again. Goombah 2 throws a hit--

Copper ducks just in time, and--

KLANG! Goombah's fist POUNDS into the lockers. Copper quickly rises, and--

Wraps Goombah 2 in a SLEEPER HOLD. Knocking him out.
Copper grabs his gun, and runs off.

Tommy turns the corner. Entering another row of lockers.
Slowly makes his way through. Gun trained in front of
him. He sees Redd's open locker. Runs inside, and--

Copper hears the OFF-SCREEN sound of PAINFUL GROANS. He
runs over, enters Redd's locker, gun drawn...

INT. STAR SAFETY STORAGE- REDD'S LOCKER- DAY

...and sees Sands. Standing over an unconscious Tommy.
Copper holsters his gun. Manages a smile.

                    COPPER COLT
          Attagirl.

Copper looks the locker over. It's EMPTY.

                    COPPER COLT
          The drugs, the cash... where is it?

Sands stands in the corner. Her head down. Remorseful.

                    SANDS MARQUEE
          ...It was supposed to be just them.

                    COPPER COLT
          What?

                    SANDS MARQUEE
          I didn't expect YOU to follow me, too...
          Didn't expect you to even CARE... Since
          when do people do that...?

                    COPPER COLT
          What're you--?

BLAM! Sands shoots Copper in the chest.

He tries to fight it. Tries to stand on his own two feet.

                         204

He can't. Collapses. Sands walks over to him, sees him writhe in pain...

...and puts her hand against his cheek. The mere touch takes all the pain away.

>   SANDS MARQUEE
>   ...shhh...

She looks at his face. For the first time, it hits her: He's beautiful.

>   SANDS MARQUEE
>   You really ARE different...

She returns his badge to his waist, and walks off. Leaving Copper with Tommy. She closes the door, locking them inside, as we...

>   FADE OUT

INT. HOSPITAL- NIGHT

Copper sits on the bed. Shirtless. A black and blue BRUISE right in the middle of his chest. Bigger than before. His shirt and Kevlar vest on the chair next to him.

Capt. Morgan and Finn stand in front of him. Deafening silence, until:

>   CAPT. MORGAN
>   That everything?

>   COPPER COLT
>   Yeah, that's... that's everything.

Capt. Morgan and Finn share a look. Both agreeing.

>   CAPT. MORGAN
>   You do understand this doesn't look
>   too good for the investigation into
>   you.

                    COPPER COLT
        I understand, sir.

                    CAPT. MORGAN
        Had you come clean about this from the
        start, when she grabbed your badge...
        this would've turned out differently.

                    COPPER COLT
        I know, sir.

                    FINN DAGGER
        Well, why DIDN'T you?

Beat. There are no words to properly answer that. All
Copper can do, is tenderly rub his bare left ring finger
with his thumb.

                    CAPT. MORGAN
        You're on a desk from here on out. If
        you survive the Internal Affairs
        investigation, THEN we'll see about
        putting you back on the street. We
        clear?

                    COPPER COLT
        Crystal, sir.

Capt. Morgan walks out, leaving Copper with Finn. Finn
goes in closer. Sniffs the air.

                    FINN DAGGER
        Smell that? That's a river of horsecrap,
        sweetheart. Careening around your
        feet. Pulling you in. Hope you've got
        the boots for it.

Finn takes his leave as well. Copper sits alone. Silent.

INT. SANDS' APARTMENT- LIVING ROOM- NIGHT

A KNOCK at the door.... And another...

KROOM!! Copper KICKS THE DOOR OPEN. Enters. No one's home. He searches. Bathroom, kitchen, bedroom-- nothing.

Back in the living room, he paces. Frustrated. Thinks out loud.

> COPPER COLT
> What're you doing?... What're you DOING,
> what do you WANT..?

He sits on the couch. Right where Sands sat when he was last here. He thinks. THINKS.

Boom. Lightbulb. Copper pieces it together. Quickly heads out.

INT. THE JOINT- NIGHT

Sands walks over to S.T. Valentine's table, clutch and LARGE DUFFEL BAG in hand (the same that Redd stole). She plops the bag over by him, interrupting his dinner. Takes a seat.

> S.T. VALENTINE
> This it?

> SANDS MARQUEE
> This it.

> S.T. VALENTINE
> Was that so hard? All this running,
> lying, and sneaking... Broads-- always
> gotta go and make things complicated.

Valentine returns to his meal. Sands sits still. After a beat, without even looking at her:

> S.T. VALENTINE
> Unless you plan on taking my plate
> back, we're done here.

Sands does not move. Her eyes, hating him. Burning holes into him. She goes for her clutch, and--

                    COPPER COLT (O.S.)
          Sands!

Copper hurries over. Sands doesn't even turn to look at
him. Her eyes NEVER leave Valentine.

                    S.T. VALENTINE
          Who's THIS clown?

                    COPPER COLT
          Police. Lemme see your hands.

                    S.T. VALENTINE
          You ain't got no cause, Dickie. Crawl
          back wherever you came from.

                    SANDS MARQUEE
          How'd you find me?

                    COPPER COLT
          "Nothing's more hidden than the
          obvious". The drugs and the cash...

EXT. WAREHOUSE- NIGHT (FLASHBACK)

In his cat burglar outfit, Redd runs off with a large
duffel bag on his back. Accomplished.

                    COPPER COLT (V.O.)
          ...Redd hid them ACROSS THE STREET
          from the FBI warehouse, didn't he? The
          last place anyone would ever think to
          look.

He runs across the street. Stashes it under a GUTTER GRATE
behind a dumpster. Covers it with trash and boxes.

INT. THE JOINT- NIGHT

                    COPPER COLT
          You knew where it was the whole time.
          You were just stalling.

                    SANDS MARQUEE
          I look like I need the money?

                    COPPER COLT
          No. No, this was never about the money.
          This was about holding on long enough
          to get Tommy Gat and his cronies off
          your back. Spin a lie about needing to
          break into a police station, and leave
          a trail to the storage locker so you
          could take them out. All so you could
          sit down with Valentine. All alone.

Sands pulls her REVOLVER on Valentine, the EXACT SAME
TIME Valentine pulls HIS GUN on her. Copper's hand is on
his holstered gun, trying to diffuse, not wanting to pull.

                    COPPER COLT
          Sands! You've jerked me around. You've
          played me for a fool... I get it.

Sands scoffs.

                    COPPER COLT
          No, I DO. I understand.

Sands readies to pull the trigger on Valentine. Copper's
got one move left:

                    COPPER COLT
          You still sleep on the far side of the
          bed, don't you?

That takes her by surprise. "How could he know that?"
Sands takes her eyes off Valentine for a HALF-SECOND,
and--

klik! Valentine drops the hammer on his gun.

Copper quickly PULLS his.

                    COPPER COLT
          Hey! COOL IT, dirtbag!

                    S.T. VALENTINE
          You're an officer of the law, and this
          broad's got a Roscoe in my face,
          threatening my person. You gonna step
          in, or do I have to defend myself?

                    COPPER COLT
          Keep quiet!... Sands? Sands, LISTEN to
          me. SANDS!

Copper's voice FADES OUT as Sands' eyes water and quiver.
They never leave Valentine, as we...

                                              DISSOLVE TO

EXT. BEACH- NIGHT (FLASHBACK)

Sands and Redd walk along the shore. Heavy.

                    REDD HART
          It's one last job.

                    SANDS MARQUEE
          It's dangerous.

                    REDD HART
          No more so than any other I've pulled.

                    SANDS MARQUEE
          It's the MOB, Redd.

                    REDD HART
          It's a CREW. Just Valentine and three
          guys.

He gently takes her by the shoulders. Hands caressing her
arms.

                    REDD HART
          It's our way out. Enough for us to grow
          old on. Build a family with.

                            210

                    SANDS MARQUEE
          We don't need the money.

                    REDD HART
          We do. THEN we'll be fine. Trust me.

Sands sighs. There's no stopping him. She takes off the
YARN BRACELET from her wrist. Puts it around his.

                    SANDS MARQUEE
          This one last job.

                    REDD HART
          One last job.

                    SANDS MARQUEE
          Stick to me, baby.

                    REDD HART
          Only til forever.

She rests her head against his chest, and we...

                                        DISSOLVE TO

INT. THE JOINT- NIGHT

Tears stream down Sands' face. Her eyes are sobbing, but
every other part is cold. Determined.

                    SANDS MARQUEE
          Believe it or not... if you want
          something kept safe, you give it to a
          thief. No one knows security better
          than them.

The pain inside BUILDS.

                    SANDS MARQUEE
          He was my everything. I GAVE HIM my
          everything. Things I'd never given
          another man. And you took him from me.
          RIPPED HIM AWAY. I wanted something

you loved. I wanted it bloody, I wanted
its head on a pike, and I wanted it as
high up as I could get it-- a WARNING
for all to see. But, since you went
ahead and gave your own son the long
kiss goodnight...

She laughs. Softly. "How could I have missed this?"

                    SANDS MARQUEE
          ...Your boy didn't mean ANYTHING to
          you, did he? Well... thank you, just the
          same.

                    S.T. VALENTINE
          For what?

                    SANDS MARQUEE
          For showing me what you value most.
          For showing me EXACTLY what I need to
          take away.

Beat. It takes Valentine a moment. As soon as he realizes--

klik! Sands drops the hammer on her gun.

Valentine tightens on the trigger, and-- BLAM!

COPPER FIRES FIRST.

Valentine slumps in his chair. Falls to the floor. Dead.

Copper and Sands are frozen. Looking at Valentine's body.
Copper's seen blood before. This is the first one on his
hands. After a long, silent beat...

Sands rises from the chair. Copper trains his weapon on
her.

                    COPPER COLT
          No. This ends NOW. I'm taking you in.

                    SANDS MARQUEE
He had a weapon, detective, and was
ready to use it. You took action.
Shoot's clean.

                    COPPER COLT
I don't care. No more dancing around--
I'M TAKING YOU IN.

                    SANDS MARQUEE
Back at my apartment. Why did you want
me to trust you?

                    COPPER COLT
What?

                    SANDS MARQUEE
Why did you need me to--

                    COPPER COLT
That has nothing to do with--

                    SANDS MARQUEE
From here on out, it DOES. Why did you
NEED ME to believe you weren't dirty?

It pains Copper to say this:

                    COPPER COLT
...Because everyone thinks I am.

                    SANDS MARQUEE
You take me in, and I'll admit I broke
in the station. I'll admit I shot you.
Admit I did the job for Valentine, that
I worked for him. And convince them
you do, too.

                    COPPER COLT
Sands...

                    SANDS MARQUEE
Take me in. And I'll make everyone's
suspicion your reality.

                            213

Copper feels as if he's been shot again. Broken.

                    COPPER COLT
          Why... why would you...? All I've done,
          all I've BEEN doing... was try to help
          you.

As coldly as she can:

                    SANDS MARQUEE
          I never asked you to.

Sands grabs the duffel bag of drugs and money. Heads for
the exit. Copper scoffs. Can't believe it.

                    COPPER COLT
          Was THAT what this was all for?

                    SANDS MARQUEE
          Already asked you: I look like I need
          the money?

She walks out. Leaving Copper with Valentine's body.
Murder weapon in his hand.

INT. PRECINCT- CAPTAIN'S OFFICE- NIGHT

Copper sits, head down. Capt. Morgan sitting before him,
at his desk. Behind Copper is Finn, pacing as he paints
his picture.

                    FINN DAGGER
          The way I see it... he's a crooked Dick
          who figured his only way out from
          under investigation was to tie up
          loose ends: Kill the only person who
          could finger him as an accomplice to
          his dead partner's crimes. Detective
          Copper Colt fired his weapon for his
          own filthy self-interest-- killing
          S.T. Valentine to save his hide. Not
          only is he DIRTY, not only is he a

DEGENERATE... but now he's a MURDERER
as well.

Beat. Capt. Morgan looks at Copper. Waiting.

                    CAPT. MORGAN
          Jesus, Copper, the hammer's coming
          down. I wanna help you, I wanna get you
          outta this... but, you gotta give me
          SOMETHING.

Copper gives nothing. Says not a word. Doesn't move an
inch. Capt. Morgan sighs.

                    CAPT. MORGAN
          Detective Colt, due to recent events, I
          am hereby placing you on suspension
          with no pay, effective immediately,
          pending the completion of Detective
          Dagger's investigation.

Copper nods. Rises from the chair, and--

                    FINN DAGGER
          Nah-uh. Gun and badge, sweetheart.

That hurts. Copper eats it. Takes off his gun and badge.
Places it on the desk. Finn smiles.

                    FINN DAGGER
          Wouldn't want you to eat a bullet like
          Sticky did, now would we? Maybe your
          aim's better and you'd get it done with
          one pull.

Copper seethes at the jab. Turns to Finn, and--

INT. PRECINCT- BULLPEN- DAY

Hustle and bustle. All is as it usually is until--

--FINN DAGGER IS THROWN THROUGH THE WINDOW OF CAPT.
MORGAN'S OFFICE. Dead silence.

Copper opens the door, and exits. Leaving the shattered glass, the unconscious Finn, and the shocked faces of his fellow officers behind him as we...

                                        FADE OUT

EXT. STREETS- DAY

Despite everything, the day is bright. Calm. The Sun mocks us wretched mortals.

INT. GREEZY SPOON DINER- DAY

Copper sits at a booth. His back to the door as he eats his breakfast. No longer on duty, he wears a simple white T-shirt. As he eats:

                    SANDS MARQUEE (O.S.)
               Whoever said clothes make the man, was
               misinformed.

Copper recognizes the voice. Sands takes the seat across him.

                    SANDS MARQUEE
               It's the other way around.

Copper doesn't bother to look up from his plate.

                    SANDS MARQUEE
               They went easy on you, all things
               considered. I half expected them to...
               what do you boys call it? "Throw the
               book at"--

THWAM! Copper SLAMS his hand on the table, shutting her up. He tries. Tries so hard to contain his anger. His pain.

                    SANDS MARQUEE
               Copper... Copper, I--

                    COPPER COLT
S.T. Valentine. Tommy Gat. Christ, even
Redd-- EVERY Joe you ever knew played
you for a sap.

                    SANDS MARQUEE
                    (offended)
Redd NEVER--

                    COPPER COLT
SHUT UP. Yes, he did. "One last job"?
"One last--" you actually FELL for
that broken tune? How many "one last
jobs" you think Redd pulled before he
met you? How many "one last jobs" you
think Redd WOULD'VE pulled if Tommy
didn't sneeze on the trigger? Everyone
you ever knew played you, lied to you,
slapped you around, shot at you... but
ME? I stuck my neck out. I put my name,
my life, my BADGE on the line for you,
you snakeskin sack of Judas. And you--

Copper cuts himself off. Laughing at himself. "I deserve
this." His pain never fades.

                    COPPER COLT
You hurt me. Not the gun you've been
waving around. Not the two bullets you
launched at my chest. YOU. YOU hurt me.

She looks deep into Copper's eyes. It makes him
uncomfortable. He tries to break away, but she holds it.
Finally:

                    COPPER COLT
What're you doing?

                    SANDS MARQUEE
I want you to see me.

                    COPPER COLT
For what?

                    SANDS MARQUEE
          For who I am.

Copper looks at her. Really looks at her. And the idiot
falls for her all over again.

Sands glances down at his left hand. His thumb tenderly
rubs against his bare ring finger.

                    SANDS MARQUEE
          Who was she?

Copper looks down at his own hand. Realizes what he's
doing. Smiles at the memory.

                    COPPER COLT
          Arial Black was a woman.

INT. BROWNSTONE- DAY (FLASHBACK)

Arial sips her coffee. Standing by the window, wearing a
men's shirt. Copper's. A cool breeze caresses past her skin.

                    COPPER COLT (V.O.)
          Soft hands, and glistening arms. Sweet
          shoulders that tasted like maple, and
          full breasts that melted when you held
          them.

Copper comes up behind her. Kissing the back of her neck.
Arms around her waist.

                    COPPER COLT (V.O.)
          A smile that could soothe, and eyes...
          eyes of...

She turns to him. He stares into her eyes. Warm. Filled
with light.

                    COPPER COLT (V.O.)
          ...hope.

Copper kisses her forehead. Tenderly.

                    COPPER COLT (V.O.)
          Arial Black was a WOMAN. But more than
          just the physical sense.

BEDROOM. Copper and Arial have a pillow fight. Laughing.
Carrying on. Feathers fall like snowflakes.

                    COPPER COLT (V.O.)
          She healed me with her touch. Wrapped
          me with her love. Made me dizzy with a
          laugh, and made me believe with every
          glance.

LATER. Arial in bed. A white bed sheet across her cocoa
skin. Copper's hand reaches in to trace the outline of her
neck. She kisses his hand as she looks at him-- at US. And
we fall in love just as well.

                    COPPER COLT
          Don't you go nowhere. You hear me?

                    ARIAL BLACK
          I hear you.

                    COPPER COLT (V.O.)
          Arial Black was a woman. Arial Black
          was MY woman.

They link hands. Copper's WEDDING RING, bright and
beautiful as we...

                                        DISSOLVE TO

INT. GREEZY SPOON DINER- DAY

Copper's hand sits ring-less on the table. Empty.

                    COPPER COLT
          She died. Mugging gone wrong. They
          wanted the ring I gave her. Feisty
          little minx gave 'em more than what
          they bargained for. Feisty, foolish
          little minx.

Sands is touched by Copper's story. She may be the only one who truly understands.

> COPPER COLT
> She was the first woman I'd ever been with. The only woman to ever know my touch in the night. They say that's the most you can share with someone, but... then I pulled the trigger.

Beat. Sands could apologize for Valentine... but knows "sorry" would never be enough.

> SANDS MARQUEE
> Where'd you two meet?

> COPPER COLT
> Walked into the ladies room. You?

> SANDS MARQUEE
> At the precinct I worked.

They softly laugh at the similarities. Their eyes connect with a glance. Copper's fingertips reach out. Just barely touching Sands'. She softly pulls away. Copper scoffs: "AGAIN, she does this to me."

> SANDS MARQUEE
> Why?

> COPPER COLT
> Why not?

> SANDS MARQUEE
> That's not good enough.

> COPPER COLT
> That's all I have. Don't lie to me. Not again. Don't tell me you don't feel this, don't... don't put that shield up.

> SANDS MARQUEE
> Yes. I feel it. I've felt it since the first night I shot you.

Defense mechanism. Her wall's back up. Copper brushes
past it.

                    COPPER COLT
          Then let me in.

Sands laughs. Softly. It soon dies as something dawns on
her. Slowly. And she's incredulous.

                    SANDS MARQUEE
          ...You think you love me.

Copper immediately realizes how foolish this is. Dives in
anyway.

                    COPPER COLT
          I know I want to.

Beat. Sands just looks at Copper. This poor, poor man.

                    SANDS MARQUEE
          Define "love". Go ahead. Define it. If
          someone's face, name, or even the touch
          of their lips pops into your mind...
          you're screwed. For the sole reason
          that every single person on the face of
          this earth will one day die, you are
          screwed. They will die, and all you'll
          be left with is their face, their name,
          and the overly-romanticized memory of
          their lips. Lips you will never touch
          again. You will grieve. You will cry.
          You will mourn. And then, you'll
          remarry. Re-engage. Re-love. Then, the
          next time you hear the word "love", you
          will think of someone else. Someone
          else's face. Someone else's name.
          Someone else's lips. And the second
          person you abandoned the memory of
          your first love for... will eventually
          abandon the memory of you, and love
          someone else.

Her words-- so precise, so cold-- wound Copper. Deep. He

tries his best not to let it show.

                    SANDS MARQUEE
          You expect me to say something
          profoundly beautiful about love.
          Truth is... I honestly don't know the
          first profoundly beautiful thing
          about it. No one does. Not even you.

Sands gets up. Heads for the door. Copper stares at the
empty space that was once her. Fighting to stay strong.
Without turning around:

                    COPPER COLT
          Don't you go nowhere. You hear me?

Sands stops in her tracks. Pain in her eyes. Without
turning around herself:

                    SANDS MARQUEE
          Don't worry. It's only til forever.

If only he knew what that meant. She exits. Leaving Copper
alone.

EXT. ALLEYWAY- NIGHT

Sands stands by an open car trunk. A DRUG DEALER checks
the DRUGS in the duffel bag inside-- the duffel Redd
stole.

He nods. Takes them, and places in another duffle bag.
Sands opens it: CASH. She closes the trunk.

EXT. PRECINCT- NIGHT

Tommy Gat walks down the block. Still in the same clothes
we last saw him in. Just as he's about to cross the street--

ERRKS! A black car screeches to a stop in front of him. The
door opens.

                        SANDS MARQUEE
        Get in.

Tommy swallows... and gets in. The car peels off.

INT. BLACK CAR- NIGHT

Tommy sits close to the door. As far away from Sands as
possible.

                        SANDS MARQUEE
                Relax. It'd be a waste of money for me to
                kill you.

                        TOMMY GAT
                You... YOU paid my bail?

                        SANDS MARQUEE
                Yes. Granted, accident or not, you DID
                pull the trigger that killed my Redd...
                but, if you hadn't killed him then,
                let's be honest, Valentine would've had
                you kill him some other night. It's not
                YOU I want. Without Valentine, your
                crew will be a mess. You're needed to
                keep a sense of control.

                        TOMMY GAT
                So... what do you WANT?

She looks out the window. Eyeing the city that rolls past.

                        SANDS MARQUEE
                Valentine's EVERYTHING.

Tommy now understands what this was all about.

                        TOMMY GAT
                What's the plan... BOSS?

EXT. STREETS- NIGHT

The black car drives off into the murky night, as we...

DISSOLVE TO

INT. COPPER'S APARTMENT- BEDROOM- NIGHT

On his back, staring at the ceiling, Copper lies on the far
side of the bed. The other side untouched. Bare. He reaches
over and touches the empty space.

A SLIVER OF MOONLIGHT cuts through between the curtains.
The sliver falls across his left hand, his bare ring
finger. Mirroring what was once there.

Copper brings the hand to his cheek. Where Sands once
touched him. He can almost hear her voice. Soothing.
Comforting.

"shhh..."

He closes his eyes. Immersing himself in that touch.

And cries.

FADE TO BLACK

END.

Here at the end, I give special thanks to those who've been there at the beginning. To every single one who's ever read my screenplays through an email or iMessage PDF...

And to everyone who made it far enough through this book to read this page...

Thank you. From the bottom of my heart. With people like you reading my scripts...

...who needs Thaddeus Plotz?